# THE BRAVER CHOICE

*A Novel by*

*John Francis*

*Serra Books, an imprint of*

𝕷𝖆𝖓𝖙𝖊𝖗𝖓𝖆𝖗𝖎𝖚𝖘 𝕻𝖗𝖊𝖘𝖘

The Braver Choice by John Francis

Lanternarius Press, Oriskany, NY 13424

Copyright 2015 John Francis

For permissions contact
Lanternariuspress@gmail.com


Cover By John Francis
Illustrations by John Francis

ISBN: 978-0-9839758-8-5 paperback

# TABLE OF CONTENTS

➢

# Chapter I: In the Beginning

From the darkness erupts the sound, a herald, the trumpet, and the funeral march begins. The light of the rising sun pierces the darkness and morning twilight engulfs the east as the snows of winter glisten from the rooftops to the dirge's beat.

A black boot is laced up tightly, and the leather squeaks in pain. A tie is made rigid and straight; like a noose. The green painted room is illuminated by one lonely lamp, standing sentinel in the darkness. The collar is lowered to press against the white shirt underneath, and out the window, the sun continues to rise and the snow sparkles. A blue trench coat is buttoned down with the belt round it fastened for a journey. A worn black gun on the bed is raised by brave gloved hands to the temple where it presses its cold black steel against the flesh. Looking into the mirror, into one's eyes, into one's soul, the trigger is pulled and the click is heard. The eyes, those deep brown eyes do not flinch at all. The gun is flung madly aside and eyes turn to see the magazine lying still and quiet on the bed; filled with hollow points of pain. Eyes, lonely eyes, peer down now into the cold black darkness, the abyss of this lowly pathetic life.

The cold of winter besets us, at a lonely seat with eyes closed and a deep chill going down the spine. The nose is runny and the hands cold with feet numb down below. There are no thoughts but only the sensation of a cold breeze running by your face and pushing against your clothing with that persistent chill. You shiver once more and awake. You open your eyes and see nothing before you, other that the cold gray pavement, shrouded in a transparent sheet of snow. Looking around you see the bus stop in this town, one beneath a metal and glass shelter. A large red brick church is in front of one, and on this side of a large avenue, a library behind you, also of red brick. Buildings are out to one's left with a few homes on the other side of the intersection to the right. The trees, stripped bare of their leaves, reflect the golden hue of the sun as they sway a gently in the passing breeze with little noise. A bitterly cold wind chill gnaws away at your face like a thousand little teeth, the fangs of winter's little pet piranhas. Now look upon the self and see the navy-blue trench coat you wear with those tan khaki pants, black boots, and nice fur-lined black leather gloves on your hands. Fix the hat on your head, tighten the scarf a bit that covers the face and ears, and fumble around those pockets for some change because here comes the bus from your left, the east. You stand now and wait as you see the approach of the bus and prepare to board, to make the first leg of your journey, the journey to answer a most distressing question, to make a most painful choice in places unknown. You wait so patiently, and shiver a while more as the noise roars from the engine of the bus and you witness its arrival, its blue and white stripes running horizontally along its sides. It stops and the doors open and you enter now from the freezing cold and into warmth, paying your fare. Into the cold unknown world, you prepare to journey with no end in sight, there is no destination specific for this winter's trip. Of course, you are not really enduring this hardship, but for Andrew Thomas Stevens, this journey has only begun.

The bus rolls on westward toward a destination unknown, and Andrew can only stare out the window and wonder about the journey ahead. He looks out and sees the passing homes of the accursed village he lives in. Further down the road, the homes thin out and soon nothing but corporate parks line the road as the signs of civilization wash away into the cold winter morning and the sun lights up the world. The boy looks around, sees the bus is still empty after all this time, and he wonders to himself if he is the only person left alive, save for the anonymous bus driver. He looks out again, sees the emptiness of the world, and thinks to himself, "It is only me now, with all my demons along for the ride." He sits back and looks out once more at the rest of the world in its emptiness, and his eyes grow heavy. He leans his arm against the window and puts his head down upon that meager platform. His eyes shut now.

A loud voice yells out from the front of the bus, "Last Stop, Spring and Waller, Ossining!" The boy wakes. A great many footsteps make themselves heard and Andrew picks up his head to see where he is. He was worried that he might be lost, but remembered that he was only in Ossining, on the somewhat familiar, "other," side of the county. He got up quickly and stepped out of the bus into the freezing cold air. Looking around, he managed his way through a small crowd of people who were getting off two other buses parked there. He looked down towards a street in the city, laying his eyes onto a group of old brick face buildings that were by a street that sloped gently downhill. He began walking through the streets on this empty morning to the places he remembered, for he had been there many times before, doing parades and visiting friends. The hill became steeper as it began to overlook the more industrial sections of town; they lay on either side of the tracks from Sing-Sing prison to Croton-Harmon station, about two more miles to the north. He walked down the road and made the left down toward the station where there was a lodge and parking lot at either side. As he continued down, he began walking along a cliff from which the road had been hewn, and looked to his right through some woods down into a running creek a good fifty feet below and felt himself entering a new land, a new world. The cities would soon turn to woods, cliffs, mountains, and wild streams of cold water. It was fascinating to see this world in a light blanket of snow, as all the distracting colors of autumn have long since faded, and now winter snows have become the reality. Suddenly there was just too much traffic for any more reflection as trucks now started to move up and down the street. Andrew was being distracted by the noise, and wandered out into the middle of the street where a loud horn from a truck startled him back into attention and he quickly moved out of its way, his coat billowing wildly in the wind of its passing. He cheated death, not ending up as road kill. Andrew regained his composure, thinking that would have been an anticlimactic death if his senses did not compel him to get out of the way. He continued his trek down the hill along the road. Descending the road some more, he caught a good view of the train station. Up on a platform on which an overpass runs, lays the station house under which are the tracks; beyond is the Hudson River, now being lit by the rays of the morning sun. He checked his pockets to make sure he had enough money in his wallet. He had withdrawn his meager savings the day before, and was glad he had brought his pocketknife, just in case. He felt a little more ready for the world, comforted that he had the contents of his pockets.

The cold was becoming a little bothersome, so Andrew ran up to the station quickly and jogged into the structure of iron, glass, and red brick. Inside there was the ever-prevalent odor of urine and some sweet-smelling industrial soap. The empty station, silent and devoid of life, save for the illuminated ticket window. It was eerie, so cautiously he approached. He looked around a moment and saw to his right a news stand that was closed for some reason. It was very dull, and he did overhear, outside, some commuter complain about how incredibly dead it was that morning, as compared to most mornings, yet he never saw the person. An old hag with dentures and long frizzled hair, along with a disgusting wart on her cheek presided over the window and Asked the boy harshly when he got up to it, "May I help you sir?"

Andrew was slightly startled, but the way he was dressed made him look like a more adult individual so he played along and disguised his voice a little, which he was very good at. "Yes, one way to," pausing momentarily to think of some place on the Hudson line, "Poughkeepsie."

The old hag punched in the destination, and through a machine next to the counter the ticket was dispensed, and then passed onto the boy through a slot underneath the glass. "That will be six dollars, and the first train will be at seven-thirty-six."

"Thank you very much," Andrew politely replied, but the hag, with an attitude, closed the screen on him suddenly.

Outside now, looking down on the tracks with ticket in hand from the overpass, Andrew looked out on the semi-industrial region. His eyes moved to look across the river to the woods and bluffs that lay beyond. Another horn was heard, the next train to Poughkeepsie. Andrew turned around and saw a staircase going down that went to the left-most platform, since there were about three of them leading to either New York City, Croton Harmon, and Poughkeepsie. Andrew became tense now as the train neared and he ran faster down the steps and nearing the bottom jumped onto the platform and saw the train pulling in. A conductor was sticking his head from a window on the diesel locomotive yelling, "Croton Harmon; Poughkeepsie, North! Croton Harmon, Poughkeepsie, North!" Andrew halted and crouched a little low to catch his breath, trying to breathe through his nose for fear of bronchitis. Finally, the train comes to a complete stop with a painful squeak. A buzzer is heard that is followed by the opening of the doors, and a few conductors step out to answer any questions about destinations. All this while, the foul odor of hot dusty brakes filled the air as the long box-like cars of the train halted, below each door the name of some person or place of interest is written in large bold letters in the middle of the cars. Andrew walked right up to a side door on one of the newer cars, passing a conductor who just stood around and said something about it being a long weekend ahead. From there he entered the car, looked around some, and took a seat looking out towards the west to have a nice view of the Hudson as he rode on north.

No whistles were heard but the ringing of a buzzer sounded as the doors closed, and soon afterwards the squeaking of the wheels below started and the train was in motion. It was not a very bumpy ride, thankfully, and the surroundings were rather clean, and yes, there was a small perceptible scent of vinyl with all the vinyl seating that was available. Andrew was the only person on that specific train car. It was quite lonely, but that did not matter for the boy, as he just sat back and smirked at the thought that he would be in peace for once.

The train was in full motion as it made its way north. He now felt more and more of the gentle rocking of the train, and looked out the window towards the Hudson and wondered about the odyssey that lay ahead for him on this cold winter day. The snow-covered trees across the way looked like tiny white and brown hairs on the faces of the bluffs and hills. His mind wandered about a little at the moment, thinking of school, thinking of the only things in life that seemed worth remembering, his friends. He sighed a bit as he continued to gaze out the window, dropping his attention on the shimmering waters of the cold Hudson that reflected on the stillness of this morning and the clear blue sky. A splendid thought it was indeed, that in the fury and decay of this hectic world, even in all his misery, he could find a little solace in the simple little pleasures of creation.

Gently the mighty river flowed on this morning, but there was an ever-increasing eagerness, manifested in the suddenly incarnate northerly breeze. There was a small flight of the birds, that even in this cold, danced merrily upon the skies. They swoop down upon the water and pick away at the unseen bounty that evades human eyes. Soon they pass away as the train rolls over a tiny bridge, and the river starts to recede from sight. Soon the tracks come back and a new station, more civilization.

# THE BRAVER CHOICE

# Chapter 2: Hello Old Friend

The river passes from sight now, and a small point of land juts out with a gleaming white field. The train approaches its next stop at Croton-Harmon, a major station where many of the trains depart from, either going north to Poughkeepsie or South to Grand Central terminal in the city. It is also here where many of the trains are sent to the roundhouse to be repaired on this line, and hence the increased number of tracks. Out the window lay a bunch of brick buildings that house the workshops where the trains are maintained. Out here is also a change in trains since there is no third rail as you head up towards Poughkeepsie, two counties away.

There would be no change of trains for Andrew as his train was the good old diesel electric kind. He began thinking about a nice camping trip he could take with a few buddies later this spring, if he made it that far. He hung his head low and lamented over how much worse life could get; how much lonelier it could get. He felt almost like crying but caught himself. It was embarrassing, even if there was nobody in the train. He loathed in a way being a nobody, and a lonely one at that, "I can't get anything done and my life is such a waste. Everything I love is passing away with one death after another. I am left with all I loathe and hate and nobody, nobody, to understand and help. I can't get out of this damn world alive. I wish I could be a God over this. I want there to be something more to this, 'life'."

The train came to a complete stop, and again the buzzer rang as the sound of opening doors was heard all throughout the car. Andrew stared out the window and looked again at a station full of people shivering in the cold winter wind that seemed to just kick up. It was particularly brutal in a frozen marsh like Croton-Harmon that is flat and vulnerable to the northwestern winds of winter. They drew up little wisps of snow that looked so much like little ghosts gliding along the ground that would go until they crashed up against some object, dissipating in a small cloud of nothing. Andrew laughed to himself as he was thankful he was not out there, and marveled at how people could just stand around like this, some of them not even dressed for the occasion as they stood there, shivering. In the mist of this icy comedy, he saw walking right past the car, a friend, one he was close to that lived in this town. He began calling out his name and banging on the window. The friend who was dressed well for this weather in his blue heavy coat and knit cap turned right to see who was banging on the window, and noticed it was his friend. The friend, ran into the car where soon he appeared inside and looked to see his friend sitting nice and comfy in a seat and motioning for him to come sit next to him.

"Andrew, what the hell are you doing here?" exclaimed the friend.

"Brian, I should ask you the same," Andrew replied in his laconic style.

Brian made a facial gesture and came trotting right over to where Andrew was sitting and took a seat as Andrew turned to look out the window again. "So, um, what are you doing here Andrew, and what's with the threads," Brian more softly asked.

Andrew turned back to speak to his friend, "I should be asking you that."

"Well, I happen to be going up to Cold Spring to pick up something for my mother since she is sick right now and doesn't want to drive there today, and I can't blame her. Although I would rather be at home, tormenting my little sister over the computer. What's your story crazy man?" Brian made a gesture of confusion and gave his ticket to the conductor who just walked by as the buzzer rang again and the doors closed.

"That's nice; now make sure you don't get stuck up there at the fair like we did last year when we went up there with your cousin."

"Yea, that was not too good, but the only difference this time is that I would freeze to death." Brian looked around out of habit and then asked the question for the fourth time, "So anyway Andrew, what the hell are you doing here?"

Andrew just put a smirk on his face and answered him assuredly, "I am going up to Poughkeepsie!"

Brian just rolled his eyes around and asked his friend in a confused way as the train went into motion, "Ugh, why are you going up to Poughkeepsie, especially on a day like today? It just seems a little odd; no offense but-."

"I have a camping trip."

"Okay, a camping trip."

"Yea!"

Brian looked around to see if he had any baggage or anything, and looked at his friend and asked him, "With who and what gear?"

Andrew again gave him a very self-assured statement with that patented smirk of his and a touch of sarcasm; "I am going it alone with nothing but the clothes on my back and my wits. It's a nice way of making a man out of myself."

Brian seemed to be even more confused as he sensed his friend having gone mad. "Okay, you know that you are going to freeze to death."

"But don't worry, I have developed the bad habit of surviving when I shouldn't. So, don't be too alarmed about it. You know I have the right survival skills and enough in me to kill a few creatures for sustenance."

"Yea, but that was with a rifle and cross bow. You don't seem to have any of that with you now."

In imitation of some intellectual, Andrew went off, "Well you must have the will to survive Brian, or else you are not worth living. If you are weak and cannot stand to fight, then what good are you? You choose to live and do what you must, for that is your will. If I choose to live, then I will do everything in my power to prove that I want to live, and try my damnedest to survive, and eventually I shall triumph. If I choose to die, then I die. 'Seek and ye shall find,' says the Lord and I believe that." Andrew sarcastically remarked to his friend in a rather pompous, and very phony way.

There was a pause and Brian spoke, "You're crazy, since the day I meet you in the beginning of freshman year, and this is only proof of that. I must have heard your grams say that speech a million times."

"Ah, you, and all others, don't understand," Andrew said assuredly, almost in imitation of a professorial type, but, with a somewhat sad look on his face before he put that smirk back on his face, and the two looked at each other and laughed.

The train continued to chug along on the tracks up to its next stops of Cortlandt, Peekskill, and what not, on the way up to Cold Spring, against the beautiful backdrop of towering cliffs and the magnificent Hudson River. The bluff across the waters came closer and the river became narrower. Past Peekskill, the Bear Mountain Bridge came into view, which allows the travelers to cross the water into the lands beyond came into view. A small island stood in the middle of the waters where a farm of sorts stood with a wonderfully quaint white field that seemed so pure. All around the mountains look down, ever watchful like the faces of unshaven men with their faces covered in snow. In this river valley there was much frivolity in the talk of the boys as they spoke about school and their many misadventures, but still there remained the puzzling question of what each one was to do at their respective locations. Over the intercoms of the train, the calm conductors voice could be heard announcing the next stop, "Garrison, next stop is Garrison."

"So what the hell are you going to do out here in this weather? Aren't you afraid of any bears or something Andrew?" Brian questioned his suddenly quiet friend who could only just stare out the window. "Um, Andrew, do you hear me?" Brian persisted.

Turning suddenly to look back at his companion, Andrew gestured his face a tad with looks of perplexity and spewed out his thoughts in response to his friend. "Brian, do you ever ask yourself about the purpose of life?"

"No," Brian replied in a sarcastically confused manner.

"Well, I do and I am a little concerned about what the fuck is going to happen to myself. If you guys had only the slightest clue as to how bad things are for me right now, you'd understand!" Andrew replied, getting a somewhat out of control halfway through.

Brian stared at his friend and was taken aback by his friend's extremely uncharacteristic outburst. "Whoaoooooo there buddy, just calm down a little there Andrew, People are going to start staring at us as if we were some sort of psychos or something. Well maybe not me, since I am sane, but Andrew-?"

"But nothing! I am just a little stressed out. So then, just let me calm down a little."

"That's good, let us just mellow out."

"Mellow?"

"Right. Let us relax and calm down before they drag us both away in strait jackets."

Andrew almost chuckled at that point, but instead he gave a comedic smirk as he rose a little from his seat and looked around and told his friend, "What people, Brian?"

"What do you mean," Brian asked, annoyed, and got up as well to look around and saw that they were the only people in the car. "What the hell is this, there are no people in this train," Brian exclaimed, rather perplexed as he sat back down.

"I guess the whole world is scared of you Brian," Andrew

told his friend quite candidly.

Brian, with a mean look in his face boldly told his friend, "Yea, they all better be afraid or else I'll go beat them all up."

"No, it's because you are so damn ugly that everybody turns to stone or drops dead; whichever one is most convenient for them." Andrew told him again, but more laconically as the train stopped and the buzzers rang with the openings of the doors.

Annoyed, Brian retorted to his friend, "Oh sure, I am so ugly. Then if I am so damn ugly, why do all the women continue to come to papa?"

"Then why don't you have a girlfriend yet?" Andrew humorously asked his now worked up friend.

"Well, well, I'm working on it you know. Sooner or later a lucky lady will come by and I'll tap that."

"It's unlucky lady."

"Oh shut up. By the way, what about Caroline? Have you asked her out yet?" Brian sadistically injected into the conversation.

Like a stake through the heart, Andrew was struck with the topic he did not want brought up for all he could do is deny the already known. "Brian, do you have to talk about her? I mean, she is old news and all-."

"Ah, I sense a little denial there buddy."

"No, but every time women are brought up, you have to talk about her," Andrew said as he tried to downplay it a little.

"Ah ha, don't try to change the subject because I know you want her."

"Everybody wants her Brian."

"I know that, but not as much as you."

"Come on, she is too reclusive and what not."

"Oh, you know if she said, 'fuck me now,' you would be like a rampaging sex- crazed sailor who would impale that ass with your battering ram of luuuv."

Andrew started to sweat a little under the collar, but hung on in with the conversation, "Yea, but so would you and every other hetero male and lesbian on earth."

"Yea, I would, but nobody wants her as bad as you," Brian persisted, sticking his finger on his friend's chest.

The train continued to chugged along, but when the train went under an overpass, that quickly darkened things for a moment. Andrew looked down toward the ground at his trusty pair of boots and then raised his head boldly and decided to level with his friend. He fixed his tie, straightened up his back, quickly threw his back against the seat of the train, and told his friend the truth. "Okay, I like her, you may say I have a little crush on her, and yes, I sometimes wish I could fuck the living shit out her, but I cannot! Not the part about liking her, or fucking the living shit out of her, but all of it. I don't want to be bothered by feelings, I just want to go on, but I can't! I'm fucking crushed by her! There, I have said it! Now is the whole God damned, motherfucking, cock sucking, world happy?"

Brian was again taken aback and more confused than ever over his friends seemingly more erratic outbursts; all of it a side he never saw of his friend before. Brian looked around some more as he was getting nervous now, as he was worried that his friend might get a little too flaky, but Cold Spring was fast approaching.

The tension was followed now by a deafening pause as

Andrew just looked at the seat cover and turned his head suddenly again to stare out the window and began to speak a little on Caroline Nisoyen.

"Brian, she was such a nice girl from the first time I ever saw her. That day when we were over at Chris's house, we met her down by the corner when I first came up to this side of the county to visit. She was so nice with that pretty, red coat and that black skirt with the black pantyhose. Man, she has great legs, and when I saw her again the following week, I bore witness to the body, and I mean the fucking body man, at the party with that tight ass dress she had on. God, I tell you, looking at her is an instant hard on, but that was not the killer because I have seen my fair share of girls who can do that to you, especially the ones form Good Kennel. No, no, it was something you don't know about, about the day in October when we had that big storm and I got stuck at Croton-Harmon when you were away."

"Yea, I remember that. We went to the hospital cause my grandpa had gallstones and I forgot to tell you not to come over," Brian softly and attentively told his friend as he listened on.

Rolling out of his mouth with great discomfort, "Yea, I remember that, but it was her again. I walked out into the town and stopped at a pizza place to wait for the next train, and there right next to me was her. I sat down and she came over because she recognized me and was rather good with me. Can you believe that she came on over to talk with me? You and everyone else knows how she can be. We talked as the wind howled outside and the rains came down like rocks, but she wanted to talk mostly about computers because her dad was thinking of getting one and she knew that I am a computer whiz and shit." A pause ensued as the train suddenly jolted and seemed to slow down. "She listened to me and did not make fun of me or anything like that. She did not make fun of the music I like, and was all right with all my friends and shit. God, she was awesome, and was like a friend, but soon her friends came and they shut me away from her. All I was left to do was to drown my sorrows in a soda and a shitty slice of pizza. Yet I am being crushed by her, but I can't stop thinking about her, especially with all the shit going on."

"But why?" Brian asked.

"Cause, there is so much I have to do, so much I could have done, but now I have her as a ghost haunting me. I don't know what it is Brian, I have seen something, I have seen something big. I have seen this choice, like a fork in the road where both ways seem too tough for me and I don't know what to do. I wish I could turn back the clock for everything and make my lot better. Why? Why? You must think that I'm on crack or something, but it's just one of those things I always think about but say nothing 'cause the whole damn world would think I am loony or something, or worse yet, not even listen."

Silence gripped the two for a while, as there was a sense of mourning over something, but what, who knows? The train rolled right along and got on over to Garrison and then on further a little more to Cold Spring as the terrain got more mountainous and the Hudson narrower. West Point came into view and the boys talked a little history, about the past, present, and future. The conversations waned quickly as Brian dutifully respected his friend's inner turmoil, but also to help him figure out the solution the only way he could, on his own. If he wants to get over her he has to think about it on his own and not defend it in any way. And if he wants her, well, why doesn't he ask her out cause as far as he knows, she's seeing no one right now. So, the time goes on and the valley looks down upon them.

"Cold Spring, Cold Spring station," spoke the voice of the Conductor from the intercom.

Brian realized it was time to part with his friend, but in him there was the feeling of finality to it all that stemmed from his friend's declared adventure ahead. He smelled death in the air and he was worried by it. His friend was not acting like his old self. Andrew was always well-spoken and quite the joker. He collected what he had on him and got up to go to the door and then spoke to his friend again in a departing tone, "Um, Stevens, be careful and just take the train back home where you belong and forget this shit. You're bugging out, bud.   I don't want you getting killed out there or hurt or something.  All right man?"

Andrew looked up to his friend with a confused and depressed look.  "All right, I'll think about it Brian, I'll think about it. I just need to get away from everything if just for a day."  The two shook hands now as the train slowed and the buzzers rang again to the tune of opening doors.

"You go take care of yourself and forget all this bullshit," Brian told his friend as he quickly dashed out towards and out the door.

"I will Brian," Andrew yelled, and then, to himself, he repeated it again in the bitterest way, "I WILL!"

The buzzers rang out again and the doors closed.  Now the train was again in motion and Andrew was now full steam ahead toward the fate awaiting for him. Life was testing him, and as he looked out the window, he saw the world.  The surrounding hills now encroached and it became darkened outside; a long hard road towards pain or eternity was ahead.

# Chapter 3: Poughkeepsie

Andrew turned away from the window and looked around to see if there were any souls around to accompany him now. There was nobody and all he could do was squirm around in his seat as he continued this journey, his choice. He wanted to let go of the past, but it would not let go of him. He wanted to let go of so much, but could not; things replayed themselves in his mind at the slightest reminder, and he could not liberate himself from them. He only wanted to run away, and he was so very good at that. Andrew was an athlete and he could run his tongue as well as his legs when need be, but cowering away from trouble felt more his way.

The sky still radiated a brilliant blue as the train continued its way north to Poughkeepsie through Beacon, hugging the beautiful Hudson nestled between the bluffs. Tugboats plod along the waters as little hamlets dot the landscape so dominated by the wondrous cliffs, all of them looming over Andrew and keeping their watchful eyes on him. Looking out the window, he saw a freight train moving up the river on the other side as the giant face of the Storm King mountain loomed over like a giant gazing down on him with its big bold face. The waters also widened now as he passed the face of the Storm King into a valley with gray misty hills beyond. An eroding castle sits on a little island close to shore. The landscape changes as Beacon is approached and more things come into view, like power plants and granaries. They looked like toys in the distance if one could almost lift up the hands and reach out to grab them. Sure enough, Andrew reached up and touched the window at these many sights, trying to grasp at something, but what? He just wanted to pass through the glass and experience the world beyond and cross the waters to the other side, something different from what he had known.

"Beacon Station, this is Beacon Station," thundered the voice of a Conductor over the intercom to snap Andrew out of it.

The train slowed down some and soon the platform of yet another station came into view as it engulfed the sights to the west. The now familiar buzzers sounded and doors were heard opening. Andrew sat still in anticipation of any who may enter, but none did into this car. The buzzer reverberated through the car again and the sound of shutting doors was heard. With the squeaking of the wheels, the train was in motion again.

Andrew sat up now and looked about to see if there was anybody around, and as before, found himself alone in the car. So then, he continued to look out the window and began to see a bridge span across the river up ahead. He wondered if he could cross this certain bridge to get to the other side and be free. His hopes grew and grew as they approached. Cars and trucks could be seen crossing the structure that was a nice cantilever bridge with a highway on top. It was a ruddy brown color that looked more like rust than paint. As the train got closer, it could be seen that this was not one bridge, but two, sitting side-by-side, high over the Hudson. But as closer examination became possible, it could be seen that there were no ways in which to cross by foot, unless a flimsy looking catwalk suspended under the Highway and nestled in the steel beams was one's idea of crossing. Andrew was a little disappointed and hoped that maybe there was another such bridge up in Poughkeepsie that could be crossed by him on foot.

Andrew had been on this train for an hour now, or more, and was wondering if he was ever going to get to Poughkeepsie. There was still one more stop at New Hamburg before he got up there. He began to stretch out a bit in his seat and yawned as he was tired after this long trip, and thought about Caroline for a second. He considered for a moment that perhaps it was all just a simple little crush and that he should not let it consume him, but no! This is an inexplicable love he has for her. He would die for her sake, just to be with her in that eternal whatever that he felt. The words hardly exist to describe his feelings for her. Besides, she is so gorgeous! Again now, Andrew became sullen by the facts, and then he began to question himself. Why was he depressed, and why did he want to cross the river? He sounded like a nut to himself now in retrospect, but again he was overtaken by the same thoughts. Perhaps there was a reason that was not merely emotional, but a sudden realization of what was one of his principle problems. He was treading water. He was running in place. He was hurrying up to wait and did nothing.

He could be home and sullen, or blow some time with a friend or two and do nothing together in a big giant circle of doing nothing. Well, he was doing something now. Instead, he was going somewhere, where, he did not know, but he was doing something, living. He stretched himself out again and stood up grasping his fist and punching the air with it, declaring loudly, "I will do this." But what was, "this?" He sat down again, sullen once more and realized that truly he had no clue what he was doing. He was drifting like one of the random sheets of ice floating down the river outside. Perhaps he really was a nut job with no direction to go.

The train again rolls on, and Andrew continued to think about this strange journey he was taking. He stares out the window with an intense curiosity about everything. He sees the river and the trees, plus the boats on the river here and there and wonders, "Is there something that made all this?" There is enough science to explain it all away as a product of Nature, but how did nature itself come about? He thought hard, but could not come to a conclusive answer as this moment of deep thought past away. He just concludes that there is a fine line between what we may consider coincidence and intelligence. As for his own life, Andrew could only conclude, "It's a fucking conspiracy."

There was a memory that came to mind. It was a rainy afternoon, years before. It was his freshman year and he was just as alone and just as miserable. He was a younger boy then, barely five foot tall. He was in a blue suit and red tie. He had this wrinkled white shirt underneath and a big old head of unkempt hair. He was outside under a bus shelter sitting on a metal bench. He was staring down on a little card. It has the picture of his Grandmother and a caption underneath, "I'm Free," and a poem underneath he could hardly remember. It was the day of his beloved Grandmother's funeral. He was alone there as the rains fell that September morning, just two and a quarter years before. A stranger sat down next to him with a time worn black guitar case. He was of average height and a strong build. He had blonde hair and a rugged workmanlike complexion. He was wearing a black leather vest with a plaid shirt underneath and a pair of blue jeans with well-worn black work shoes below. He asked him with a musical tenor voice, "So what seems to be the problem there, son?"

Andrew turned to look at this mysterious stranger and told him with tears welling up in his eyes, "Nothing, sir."

The stranger nodded his head, unsurprised and looking down, on him said to him, "Well, if there was nothing wrong, you wouldn't be holding back tears like that." He seemed to look on a bit at Andrew's hands and saw the card and replied to him, "Well there, looks like you just came from a funeral. Who was it for may I ask?"

Still holding back tears and trying to look strong, Andrew replied, "My grandma."

The stranger nodded his head and instructed Andrew, "Like the seasons we too shall all pass away at some time. Her time was now. But don't cry for her. Just live."

"Why?" the young Andrew replied.

The stranger smiled on him and said, "Because son, the purpose of life is to be lived. You only have one life. You cry for her which tells me she did good. It means she was loved, means that you love, and that is the most important thing a person can do."

"But what if I don't love anything, what if I don't love life?"

A bus was approaching and they both turned to look. The man got up and continued, "Well, if you don't love, you sure are the saddest thing in the world. If you do not love your life, then you will be one miserable person, but as long and you love, then you can be redeemed. You cry for somebody, that shows you are already no monster. Think about that." The bus stopped and the doors opened. The guitar slinger got off and nodding his head towards Andrew said, "Vaya con dios, kid."

"Vaya con Dios, kid," Andrew now repeated to himself in the train. "Vaya con dios, go with God." He smirked and continued staring out the window.

New Hamburg, a quaint little town just before Poughkeepsie, comes into view, covering up the mighty Hudson's modest vacation homes and boats tethered to shore. There was something strangely familiar about this town, a comforting familiarity. The placement of the trees, and the look of the houses, reminded him of White Plains, but particularly Stepinac. He smiled a moment at this realization and felt more comfortable, almost as if he had been going to school. Another memory flooded into the boy's mind of the annual Walk-a-thon that used to be held for fundraising, but since phased out. He was only a Frosh when the last one was held, and he, of course, remembers it as one of those more special moments. He journeyed around the neighborhood with all his newfound friends conversing and joking all the way. He misses those times that will never be again, so much possibility and hope there in the beginning. If only there was a way he could recapture them and continue to live in the feeling of those moments like a drug addict. The days were so much happier then. If time could only stop its brutal assault on him. At least there was something about life that he did love, it was those sweet cherished memories of times now gone.

The buzzer rings again, and the train is soon rolling right along on its journey to Poughkeepsie. Soon enough, the small village of New Hamburg fades away and again we return to the full view of the Hudson and now see an increase in the number of hills and cliffs along the river. Time marches on, and so does this train ride. Now on the other side of the river can be seen yet another freight train carving its way up the river on tracks so close to the water that it seems to almost skip along it like a long parade of pebbles from the distance. All these unfamiliar sights intrigue the boy as he attentively looks out at all the individual little houses and old time worn factories by the riverside. It felt like looking at ruins of Rome and Greece, of an industrial time long past. The train passes by a concrete factory, then giant storage tanks of oil along with the sudden appearance of sheer cliffs on the other side. Just now a magnificent bridge comes into view ahead. Abandoned sheds and factories now come to obstruct the view of the Hudson and more does one sense the approach of a city, and now everything seems to look just a little more familiar, in the urban sense.

A little anxious, Andrew readied himself to get off. As the bridge comes closer, Andrew is relieved even more that it does have a walkway, and what a marvelous suspension bridge it is in its ghostly gray. Further up is another bridge that is rust covered, but as the train approaches, abandoned it seems, for now. Soon enough that does not matter, for now the Hudson is suddenly covered up by fallen rocks that look more like black coal. Andrew wonders if he is entering the gates of Hell with all this black around. The train slows down to a crawl and looking out the windows only the graffiti greets the eyes. A train platform comes into view and now over the intercom comes the voice of the Conductor, "This is Poughkeepsie Station. All commuters must exit this train and transfer onto Amtrak for service to Albany, Utica, Syracuse, Rochester, Amherst, Boston, Buffalo, and Chicago. Please exit this train and check to see that you have all your bags with you when you exit. Thank you for riding Metro North Railroad, the Hudson Line. Have a nice day." The train finally came to a stop and the buzzers are heard as the doors open. Andrew, having nothing other than the clothes on his back and the contents of his pocket. A little conversation was now being heard over the intercom by the conductors who did not notice that they left the intercoms on.

31

"Bill, I have the rest of today, to work. I got a few more trips in me today." One of the Conductors plainly said.

"Yea, I got to take some vacation time this weekend," the other replied.

"Great. I got the week off after this; I am going skiing and going to get destroyed."

"Good, find me a nice rich single lady to play with, 'cause I don't have enough to party like that," Laughter is heard on the platforms and elsewhere as people are listening to this exchange.

Questioning, the other voiced asked, "Hey, why not, we'll both go up with a few of the guys; get drunk and party, and have a hell of time," And as is expected, roars of laughter are heard as the conductors carry on, not realizing that the whole world is listening their hot mic. Even Andrew can't help himself as he busts out in laughter.

"No, I can't, I gotta to pay off my alimony, and I also have surgery scheduled this week for my fucking hemorrhoids. I can't do anything all week." Yes, the laughter continues.

Finally, the other conductor realizes that he left something on, "Yea, that is too bad, and oh shit, I left this on. Hold it, I hope nobody was listening," and thus ended the conversation. Andrew was almost in tears from this little snafu of the conductors, and just made his way out of the train shaking his head.

Looking around one finds that this is a rather drab place to be with its platforms nestled below a structure that is the station house. Beyond, up to the north is what appears to be a train yard with its numerous rust red tracks whose worn tops shimmer in the sunshine that is beyond. Yet around Andrew there is nothing but the cold concrete pavement of the platforms and steel beams that support a riveted steel shelter above. Before Andrew now is a tall staircase leading up to the rest of the station, and, of course, that wonderful smell of urine permeates the environment as one climbs up the long staircase to an unknown world above. The boy looks around and tries to absorb these unknown surroundings that resemble more a rundown lavatory from the turn of the century than a train station.

Andrew got to the top of the stairs and he looked around to see nothing more than an empty room with large windows looking down upon the tracks that were shadowed by the station house. It looked like some hole in a dusty and dirty steel mill in there with all the rusty iron showing. He looked right and saw light, and through a group of doors what seemed to be a waiting room. With little hesitation, he moved on towards the light. With graceful steps anticipating the revelation of something wonderful, something new, and everlasting. There was a strange confidence, as if, somehow, he would discover treasure or some mysterious solution to all his troubles. Then, again, a little breakfast would do just fine as well. Ponderous steps took the boy as he came ever closer to the door, ever closer to a truth, to the sunshine, away from this gloomy room up over darkened tracks that were being lit by the light from on high. Mighty and magnificent steps approached the doors and the right hand of Andrew arose like a mighty hero from the drowning waters of failure. He surely and gracefully grabbed the handle of the door and opened it.

"Oh God, no," Andrew disappointingly said as he looked on at a business man, decked out in his dark blue suit sipping on a cup of coffee; a familiar face in a great suit but messy graying hair.

The figure lifted up his head and moved the cup away from his face and boisterously greeted the boy, "Andrew T. Stevens, so good to see you this fine morning! What the heck are you doing so far up here?"

Unenthusiastically, Andrew politely responded, "Good to see you too Mr. Blatt. I too did not expect to run into you up here in the middle of nowhere, New York."

Yes, here was the uncle of Andrew's affections, a man also capable of being very annoying and persistent on the most uncomfortable things. He continued with Andrew, "My son told me you threw a great pass to him under pressure at that big game last year against Iona."

Andrew felt embarrassed because he was wrong, and corrected him, "Um, actually, I am just a half back and your son plays on the JV. I am varsity, sir."

"Oh that's right, see what happens when you see your son only on the weekends?" Mr. Blatt sighed, "Well at least you guys are in the band together, or something."

Again, Andrew had to correct him, "actually sir, he is the choir. He left band after freshman year."

"Oh, I see, geez, I keep forgetting these things; life's nuts you know," he responded, animated and embarrassing to be around.

Andrew wanted to worm his way out and started to tell him, "Well, I got to get going I have-"

"I was just thinking about you earlier when I was talking with one of my buddies last night on how I should get my brother-in-law to, you know, hook you up with my niece because you are such a great kid with a wonderful pedigree," Mr. Blatt flatteringly told Andrew, who did not know if he should be elated or disgusted by who is trying to hook him up.

Andrew, trying to hide his embarrassment, nervously tells him, "That's nice, but you know I am busy with school and shit-"

"Oh think nothing of it," he told him in an increasingly sleazy sounding way. "She could use somebody like you in her life." He spoke as he slowed down near the   end, and became very repulsed.  A pause followed as a departing train was announced and a whistle blew when Mr. Blatt finally got serious.  "Andrew, do you know how much patience a person must live with when dealing with troubled people?  Huh?  My brother-in-law knows that all too well."

"No, I do not," Andrew incredulously replied, however now becoming intensely interested in the conversation. Then Mr. Blatt invited him to sit with him in one of the nearby wooden benches that looked like large, rounded, and glorified versions of a church pew. "Come, let us sit a while, and we'll discuss a little more about this."

"Good, my hands are getting a little shaky from holding this coffee.  That's what a little too much of this stuff will do to you."

They both walked on over a few steps to the benches and sat down together across from some more identical benches and began to talk seriously.  "So then, what were you saying about there being a little behavior problem somewhere?" Andrew cautiously asked as he turned his head with a mischievous look.

Mr. Blatt set down his coffee a moment, "Caroline is a sweet girl sometimes, but she's increasingly a handful, always getting into trouble.  David, her father is a tough man having hung in there so long.  He thought that some military-like discipline and fewer shrinks would do the trick, and I got to hand it to him, it seems to have worked for a while.  Even my son, her cousin had started to take a dislike for her."

Blatt paused a moment and Andrew had this immense

35

nervousness grab hold of his gut as something very uncomfortable was welling up inside. He produced a fake smile, "That is rather interesting, there is so much that I did not know about her."

Mr. Blatt's eyes drew together and his eyebrows went up in surprise. He asked the boy suddenly, "You know Caroline?"

Andrew, not knowing what the heck to say, twisted his face around in the motions of embarrassment and told him, "Yea, I know her. She is friends with a few kids I know and, well you figure, your son's cousin, I just hang out with people and, well, you know."

"That's interesting," Blatt said as he nodded his head around in similar perplexity as to what to say in return, but had a sudden flash of words and said, "Well, at least the news that she has some 'friends' that aren't in jail is an improvement, so I guess that's good. I think you should go out with her, because you would be good for her, make her less, well, 'crazy'."

"Sometimes the crazy have made themselves crazy," Andrew responded trying to sound smart, as all he could think about was Caroline's ass.

Mr. Blatt nodded in approval and hesitantly told him, "Yes, that is so true in reality. That is so true. You know, I think she is even up here this weekend or something, had an athletic thing over at the college that her dad probably sucked her into. Probably hanging with her other cousin or something. I dunno. Bunch of trouble makers." He had a rather annoyed look on his face now, which he rapidly dissipated in a cup of coffee. Andrew, for his part, started thinking. A sneeze was heard in the rather desolate waiting room that had become suddenly chillier, and all that could be heard now was the unremitting sounds of the cars passing over the expansion joints of Route 9. At least there was the sunshine breaking through the structures to the east.

"Well there Andrew, I got to get going," Mr. Blatt said rather carefree as he got up and picked up his coffee. "I got to work on my eye strain for the rest of today. Gosh, there are so few people out today, it is almost as if it were a holiday."

"A holiday from what?" Andrew asked from the bench.

"I don't know, guess a holiday from life. People don't care about anything. They just sit down and let the industrial entertainment complex do the talking, and then miss out on a great day like today. Oh well, I'll just go ahead and enjoy the nose bleed section of the building. See you around Andrew." He made his exit with a swift turn towards the doors that lead to that glum room and down the stairs to the tracks.

"Have a nice day," Andrew said rather unenthusiastically as he looked straight on at the bench before him. He reflected a little on what had just transpired, and on the new news about Caroline, but he did not want to go where his mind was taking him. Maybe that could drown the slight sorrows he felt in the back of his heart; in the deepest recesses of his mind, but he could not escape the truth, and he could not escape this choice he felt he needed to make. The boy just sat there and developed a pity in heart about the girl. Fantasies about taking care of her and being Caroline's protector, and what not, put a smile back on his face, along with the possibility of her being nearby. Then with a little reflection he looked up and said quite softly, "Looks like I got a chance to be her, 'man'."

Stepping out into the cold crisp air, Andrew's breath billowed before him like the steam of a locomotive and surveyed this city before him. Immediately ahead was the green Route 9 overpass with the sounds of cars trampling over the expansion joints at high speed. He started walking up a hill, a long slope upwards towards the rising morning sun. A few taxies were parked before the station, eagerly waiting like a pack of hungry yellow wolves for their feed of commuters this frozen morning, their tail pipes smoking like the nostrils of eight-cylinder beasts. Andrew walked past them and up the hill under the overpass, noisy from the traffic above. It was an interesting place, Poughkeepsie. He looked up and saw a few pigeons roosting on the beams of the overpass as the clanking sound of the expansion joints continued to fill the air from the cars driving up and down Route 9.  Ahead of him was a little hill, and on it streets that lead towards the rest of the city.  He walked on up it and ran into more city, where plenty of redbrick apartments houses lined both sides of the street.  Andrew turned right and saw an empty street heading towards the bridge he saw earlier.  He practically marched up the street like a good soldier on parade.  The small three-or-four story apartment buildings around him were not too large, but they were enough to cast their shadows on the street and darkened Andrew's path.

It was mornings like this that a young child would go outside and play against imaginary foes.  He had immersed in stories of fantasy and real history, and would pick up a stick and pretend he was fighting against an armed foe.  Bravely would the child challenge this black knight in his mind, and battle on and on till he finally slew the evil.  How on a morning like this the child would run around the block chasing squirrels or what not, and turning to run the other direction to escape the dogs, raccoons, or other children, etc.  The seasons never bothered him too much, he learned to endure the vicissitudes of the weather, and in a masochistic sort of way learned to enjoy the ravages of nature.  He did so most especially those cold winter days when he had all the great outdoors to himself.  The world was too afraid to suffer in the cold.  In life, these were for him some of the most pleasant memories in a so far dreary existence.  Spotting a suitable stick on the ground, he picked it up and saw in it what kind of a good sword it would make.  He saw a tree, that in his mind had suddenly turned into a villain bent on destroying him. Looking around to see that he was in the beginning of a residential neighborhood, he felt a little reluctant to fight this enemy; but he has a mission to accomplish and he is going to defeat this Scoundrel. He began to swing at the tree and moved around, parried, blocked and took stabs at the tree with such dazzlingly fast and efficient swiftness that anybody would be impressed. With each blow the snow would shake loose from the tree and fall around him? It glistened in the radiant sunshine that managed to sneak through a street corner in this perfectly clear morning. He swung and fought on till the stick had begun to whittle down to a mere stud of itself, pretending to block he ducked, turned to the right, and grabbed a low branch that was sticking out and broke it off, and then stabbed the tree with it before dropping it. Andrew stood there rather satisfied at his imaginary prowess and could only smile at a resurrection of old times for himself, even if it was only momentary on the scared tree bark.

Suddenly an accented voice from behind startled Andrew, "So, are you also going to the exhibition?"

Turning around to see who was speaking, Andrew saw that it was a short old man dressed in a tan leather coat and a gray wool cap; his hands were in his pocket. Andrew gave a look of perplexity at the man and asked him, "Who are you?"

"I am nobody much, I just happened to be on my way to the store. I saw you battling that tree and I thought you were practicing. There is a fencing meet in New Paltz, and I thought that was the reason behind your assaulting the tree."

Andrew continued to give another look of bewilderment and decided to press on and find out some more, "Ah, I have no clue what the heck you are talking about."

The old man deliberately told him, "New Paltz, the college there, you know-?"

"I know now," Andrew interrupted as he saw what he was

talking about.

"Okay, so I guess you just had the wonderful urge to attack the tree then," added the old man.

"Hmm, no. I just, well, I don't know. When I was a boy I used to pretend I was fighting against other swordsmen or what not, and I guess a morning like this just reminded me of those days I guess." Andrew honestly told the guy.

The old man nodded a bit, now understanding why Andrew was attacking the tree. He looked now straight at Andrew, as if he knew something but was not willing to say it, "Well then, you take care. I think you would make an excellent swordsman though, when you get the chance."

"So says my uncle," Andrew told him more comfortably.

"Your uncle has a good eye. What does he do?" asked the man.

"He is an engineer at IBM up here. I call him my uncle because he was such close friends with my father, and I grew up with him around. Takeo Ishi is his name. He seems to be quite popular around here."

"Ah, Takeo," the man said, "Yes, I know him. Excellent engineer, made many breakthroughs with IBM over the years. I used to work at the Research Center in Hawthorn, so I have heard his name many times. Well, you carry on young man, I have to make my rounds this morning and get some fish for my wife." At that the man patted Andrew on his shoulder as Andrew himself tipped his hat to him as he walked away.

Andrew was reminded of his uncle Tee as he grew up calling him. He did not live too far away, just a little bit further north in Red Hook. Poughkeepsie now seemed far more familiar to him. Uncle Tee and his wife were unable to have children, so they lavished their attention on Andrew. He spent almost every other weekend of his life, it seemed, with them, learning much from uncle, including how to fight; a thing he kept to himself tightly. Mrs. Ishi was dead now for two years and Takeo was not doing so good himself, despite being only his father's age. Perhaps behind his smile was also a very sad man, though he never showed it. Maybe that is why he does not drive down much anymore. Andrew missed that smile, like he missed so many other things, and he was not even eighteen yet. Close people already drifting away.

The bridge, looking to his right, stood sentinel like a gray ghostly gate to an unknown world. He began to walk in that direction and as he did so, he looked up to the heavens and sighed. Andrew began to look down in order not to trip over a curb and looked up again with a plea from his heart, "I just want to get IT over with."

The rays of the morning sunlight beat down on him brightly, shedding what little warmth it could on this winter day. He moved up, quickly picking up the pace and then stopped to stare as he saw something up ahead going up towards the bridge. It was a very attractive jogger, a blonde-haired beauty and tight sweat clothes, jogging up the road. Andrew stopped for a moment to admire her, but then felt himself brought low. He felt horribly conflicted. He was a good Christian boy, but he also wanted Caroline, and he also did not want to look like a weird creepy pig. He wallowed now slowly towards the bridge and began his climb, head hung low as the attractive jogger passed by. He got up to the road that crossed it and began moving with a bit more diligence. The sidewalk crossed over an overpass that had Route 9 below. He gingerly crossed over an off ramp, trying not to get run over by traffic exiting Route 9. He continued forward and finally crossed over to the foot of the bridge and began his ascent. An eerie wind again blew across the landscape and sent shivers down the spine of the boy. Silence, and the wind; that is all there is to hear at this moment. Andrew stood his ground, trembling, his eyes gazing from the bridge, to the hills around, and to the city, to the waters below. The sidewalk was salted and crackled with every step like he was walking on eggshells. He began to step forward past the giant concrete anchors for the suspension cables. Next to him the traffic lightly flowed. He walked on now over the tracks and towards the first tower. He could jump now to his death, but, somehow, he could not. It would be so easy and there were no people really to stop him, but still, he could not do it. He could not take the plunge. However, now, he had a thought return to his mind. The agony of his recent past began to kill him again like a tidal wave. He remembered the awful truth he was escaping from right now, and in his head, he felt a voice say, "Jump boy, jump, jump now!" He stopped for a moment and the wind howled strongly before it died down again, and the voice returned, "Jump now boy, run up to the railings and take a leap into eternity! Do it, DO IT NOW!" He shivered, not from the cold anymore, but from what was in his head.

# Chapter 4: Bridge across cold waters

In a narrow passage through the first gray tower there curiously echoed the sound of falling cardboard boxes. Andrew rushed a little to investigate. Walking in he saw a young girl trying to arrange a few packages for easier carry. Andrew asked her, as she was kneeling on the ground picking up the fallen packages, "Miss, do you need some help?"

The young lady, looking very much his age with long, fine blond hair, looked up at him and smiled. With a sort of winning, but sweet voice, she replied to him, "Oh, thank you, I don't know how I would manage to get these gifts across."

"Well, it would be my pleasure," Andrew politely told her, bending down to pick up some of the boxes, a little larger than shoe boxes, for boots, and all in plain brown wrappers.

The young girl looked up to him and noticed that Andrew was about her age, and puzzled at why he was dressed so fancy, "You dress real nice, what's the occasion?"

Andrew looked down at her pretty face and radiant blue eyes. She was so cute and innocent; there was nothing to fear from her. "I thought I would dress up today."

Smiling, she told him, "It looks real nice on you."

Andrew kind of blushed, feeling a little embarrassed and on the spot, "Thank you. I haven't heard that in a while."

"I'm surprised." The young lady told him as she got up. Andrew checked her out some more. The jeans fit well on her as did her purple heavy coat. He was impressed by her, though she was a bit of a small woman, even with the boots she was wearing, she was no more than five two. "I would think that somebody sooner or later would compliment you," she politely told him, with a smile.

"Yes, yes," Andrew tried to pass humbly as he could since he could not help but try to be impressive to this cutie, "And I got to say that you yourself are not looking all that bad. But heck, aside from the cold, today is so beautiful. I wish I had a camera."

"Me too?" the young lady asked in a very eager fashion.

With a twist in his face, Andrew injected a little irony in the moment, "Well let me help you across this bridge."

"Okay there, but don't run away with them boxes," the young lady told Andrew again in the most ditzy way one could imagine, her voice was naturally ditzy.

They started off walking and the young lady asked Andrew, "So who are you and what are you doing here? Do you go school in Poughkeepsie?"

"Why would you say that?" Andrew politely asked her as the breeze settled down.

"Well I don't ever remember seeing you in school. I assume you must be from the other side of the river?"

Andrew looked at her and gave a wise grin. He told her almost boastfully, "Yea, I'm from your side of the river, but way to the south. I'm a proud Stepinac boy. Westchester is my home pretty much."

The young lady looked bewildered and asked, "You're from all the way down there, so what are you doing here, on this cold day?"

Andrew looked at her again and told her more relaxed, "I'm up here just checking things out. See, me and my buddies are going camping up this way in the spring and I just wanted to check things out. It's winter break so what else is there to do?"

"You could go to the mall," the young lady replied. "They got like two of them in White Plains. I go down there sometimes to shop."

"Yea, but I've been there a million times. Hell, I've been just about everywhere. You really can't glue me down to any one place in particular except maybe school, but even then……."

The young lady was fascinated by Andrew, she asked him, "So you like to go everywhere. Have you been anywhere really exciting?"

"Yea," Andrew turned to look at her excitedly, eager like a child on Christmas morning, "Absolutely. I have been all over the world, I have visited India, Germany, France, all over South America. I even went all the way to Nepal."

The young lady stopped and her eyes opened wider still. She asked him amazed, "Are you rich or something?"

"No, my dad is well connected having been an important engineer and old Fighter Pilot. He almost became an Ace in Nam with four and a half confirmed kills." Andrew for a moment almost seemed to glow with pride. "The old pilots take such good care of each other."

"Wow," the young lady exclaimed and excitedly asked, "So what does your mom do?"

And the cold wind blew again.

Silent and still for a moment, Andrew was almost at a loss for words, the sudden good mood gone in a flash. He almost trembled when he spoke again, "She's dead, she's very dead, with my older sister. I never knew them. There're just old faded pictures from the seventies."

And, again, the wind blew.

The young lady was shocked by this startling admonition.

She was compelled to comfort this stranger, "I am so sorry. I was just curious."

Andrew tried to deflect the issue a little. It was something that he did not want to stumble into. "It's okay, I never really knew them. My dad got crippled in the accident, but my grandparents stepped in, along with a lot of others. Still pisses dad off when people assume he is in a wheel chair cause of Nam. No, it was just a stupid car accident."

Andrew resumed walking while the young lady stunned for a moment, snapped out of her little trance and now was following him. "Well I am sure your dad has done well, he sounds strong taking you all those places even though he got hurt."

Annoyed now that she was not following along closely enough because he had already alluded to it already, he answered, "His buddies, they are the ones who took me around the world."

She bravely tried to cheer him up, "I am so sorry about your family, I didn't know, I just met you like five minutes ago."

Andrew slowed down a bit and took her words into consideration. He more reflectively told her, "True. You don't know me. I'm just some stupid junior in high school walking a bridge holding a couple of boxes. I just have a lot of things on my mind, always."

"I guess that is why you like going away to places," she calmly challenged him.

Andrew smirked at her for a second, feeling a bit embarrassed, but also open. "I guess so. I guess that is why I am even here talking with you. I always hope the answer is out there somewhere, cause it sure ain't at home."

"What about school?"

Andrew laughed a little under his breath and assured her, "I have too much fun there. Lots of good times, but no real answers to my questions, or at least any that I like."

"Oh!" she exclaimed, and with more curiosity asked him, "But how is it like. I've never been there. I just know it some, from reading about the high school sports."

"We're not the jocks for every week it would seem that we get our asses handed to us on the diamond, gridiron, or gym floor. Poor nerds were we, and proud of that fact. I bet we outperform the pricier schools. Everybody knows it, but nobody seems to care much about that, they just make fun of us. I ask, 'Why does man not cherish his greatest gift, the mind?' What is it meant to be a Stepinac boy? It is to be wrongfully rejected, and alone."

Shyly, and with total heavenly sweetness, Andrew's companion looked up to him, holding the tear in her eye and imparted on him sweet kisses in words, "You're lonely, I can tell. My mother is always telling me that sometimes the loneliest people are surrounded by the most people. They just don't know you, and maybe it's your fault or not, but it brought you out here. Maybe you'll be lucky and find what you are looking for out here."

"Find what?"

"I don't know, maybe life."

She made him smile and for a moment Andrew could see her as a random hot cutie on the bridge with him, but a comforting guardian angel.

They chatted some more on the way across about nothing till they got to the end of the bridge where a little park of sorts seemed carved straight out of the rock. Beyond lay a few houses along a lonely picturesque road. Andrew had to part ways with this sweet young girl no older than himself. As they walked on to the road, she stopped to look at him, and said, "You can give me those boxes, I can take it from here. I just have a short way to go." Andrew piled the boxes he had on her arms carefully as they shared a smile together. She looked at him and said, "You are a good person. You yourself may not be that happy but you sure made my morning. I'm sure all your friends feel the same way about you."

"Perhaps," Andrew said graciously as he studied her one last time, feeling a sense of loss.

She started walking down one side road and before she vanished from sight, she turned and yelled toward Andrew from beyond, "Don't ever give up. You're a good person."

Andrew did not know quite what to make of that remark, but he knew one thing, he should have fallen for someone like her instead.

The road ahead of Andrew was going off into a wooded area that was sinister with its many trees lining both sides of this rough road, seemingly gazing down on one with its skeletal branches. He walked on as he felt the crackling of the broken pavement and

49

looked around himself. It was so contrasting. One moment there is the beautiful blonde girl, and now there is this desolate eerie road that seemed to lead nowhere.

He looked ahead and pressed on when he suddenly took a tumble. He had stepped into a pothole and twisted his foot. Fortunately, it only hurt his pride some, but still enough for him to have to hold his foot for a moment with his gloves. He stopped to straighten himself up a little and brush off the debris from his coat when he heard the breaking of branches. His head flew around, hoping it would be the pretty little beauty he had just left, but it was not. He saw nothing but more barren trees and withered bushes. He started walking again and violently asked, "Why the hell can't life just leave me alone? I have enough things to worry about, and I'm just sixteen still!"

Suddenly, there from behind was another crackle and Andrew looked back and saw amongst the dead vegetation, the biggest, blackest, and most fearsome dog he had ever seen in his life. It's white teeth shone with drool dripping from its enormous fangs to the ground below and let out a loud vicious bark. As it suddenly lunged out of the woods from less than a hundred yards away and began running after Andrew. Andrew's eyes opened in shock and he instantly began to sprint out down the road, faster and faster, hearing clearly the patter of the dog's feet. Quickly, he glimpsed a large branch on the road and picked it up and fiercely swung around, managing to hit the dog on the left side of its face before it could jump up to overcome him. The animal flew aside and staggered a little, but Andrew kept running. He kept on running and saw a road ahead of him. He flew out into the traffic, cars stopped and began honking furiously as he hit the front of a car and looked the driver in the eye and kept on running to the other side. He stopped, looked back on the other side of the heavy traffic and saw the dog staring at him with great indignation and turned away towards the woods again. Startled, Andrew turned and walked on in shock, and all thoughts emptied from his mind. His breath filled the air before him and enshrouded him in its dense fog as he continued to gaze at the dog as it disappeared back into the woods.

# Chapter 5: On the road again

Walking now alone down a busy road, a few stores and eateries presented themselves to Andrew. A donut shop that was part of a little white building passes him by and he looked forward a little more and caught sight of a fast food joint. It was open and he was sure that he might find some breakfast there to eat; he was starving at this point. He approached, walking through an empty parking lot to get there. A few cars came whizzing by and almost splashed some slush on Andrew who paused for a moment in great annoyance, but he kept on walking faithfully to his destination. Entering in he looked around and noticed that it was just your typical fast food joint with faux wooden chairs, green wall with wood trims, and of course that front counter with the whole menu up above along with ads for the new this and supersized that. Andrew studied it a bit and decided that all he wanted was an egg and cheese muffin and some coffee to go along with it. Looking to the cashier, he stated his culinary desires to the rather homely brunet on the other side. "Hi miss, I'd like to order an egg and cheese with coffee."

In a cheerfully fake way she challenged his order, as all these people are supposed to do anyway, with a suggestion for what value meal or something, "Would you like one of our value meals instead since you get-"

Andrew a little too impatient for this sort of thing rudely interrupted her, "Make it a number two."

"Okay then sir," the young lady replies as she looks back and calls out loudly, "A number two please." She then rang up the price for Andrew who already had a five out on the counter. She asked him, "You seem to not be in a good mood this morning sir?"

Andrew quite blunt told her in a menacing way, "I just got chased a good quarter mile by a neo rabid dog black dog from the fiery depths of hell, just got mud all over my father's coat, and have no clue where the fuck I am!"

From behind a sassy, female voice answered Andrew,

"Highland!"

Without looking back, the he yelled back a "thank you!"

The voice in the back giggled a bit at Andrew's answer, and all he did was look to the heavens for a moment and shake his head in annoyance. Immediately, a tray is plopped down before Andrew with his meal.

The cashier cheerfully as before acknowledges the boy, "Enjoy your meal sir." Andrew pulled away giving her a friendlier look than before and went to find himself a seat. Looking at the right corner he sees the face of the voice that gave him his answer to where he is. It was Venus incarnate. Wearing a denim shirt with tight jeans, this beauty was not of great stature, but her powerful blue eyes drew Andrew closer, and her dirty blond hair appealed to him, and to say the least she had the greatest pair of tits he had seen all day. There was a warm familiarity to her.

The young beauty spoke up to Andrew, "So you looking for a place to sit?"

Andrew was tremendously enticed by the offer, "Sure, I could use some company today."

"I can see you're lost or something up here. What the hell are you doing?" The beauty asked the Andrew who had begun to remove the lid from his coffee.

"I have no clue," he answered her as he picked up his coffee and carefully took a sip. He continued, "I'm just up here for something. A personal little something I guess."

Sharply the young lady across him on the table injected, "Cool, cause I have no clue what the hell I'm doing out here either." She paused a second and continued, "Well, I'm just trying to avoid some shit, that's all."

"What is it then," Andrew asked as he continued to sip on his coffee, and then began to open up his wrapped up egg and cheese.

The young lady gave him a dirty look as if something had struck an uncomfortable cord. She more tensely asked Andrew, "How old are you 'cause you are dressed really fancy, but have a baby face."

"Sixteen."

"A little older," the goddess replied, which awoke in Andrew a suspicion, and attraction.

Having taken a bite or two during the young lady's reply, Andrew swallowed his food and decided to take a more aggressive stance in this conversation with the stranger, "You don't sound like you are from around here, and besides, why are you having just a coffee for breakfast?"

A little more open the young lady answered Andrew, "I ate something last night at a rest stop that didn't agree with me too much. I just wanted a coffee right now, that's all."

"Yea," Andrew persisted, "but wouldn't coffee make your tummy feel worse?"

"Not for me," the young lady replied rather timidly. "I am a proud caffeine addict."

"Where are you from," Andrew asked her more authoritatively

"Upstate, about three hundred miles west or so. It was a five hour drive."

Andrew sitting back checked her out some more a second and from the suspicions in his mind told the young lady, "I knew you had to be from the 'boonies.' Your accent gave you away."

"Duh," she replied to him a very fresh way before she got back to giggling over the way she responded. "Is that what people down here would call 'ebonic sound?'"

"No," Andrew calmly replied, "But I do get the distinct impression that you are a runaway. You are just out of cash and were hoping someone would share breakfast with you, otherwise why else would you just drink a stupid coffee here. Again, Coffee would make your stomach feel worse."

She corrected him, "I got plenty of cash, a private plane at my disposal, and connections, besides, aren't you the same thing. I can tell you went to a private or parochial school, or something by the way you dress and talk."

"Right on. Besides, what does the fact that I'm from parochial school have to do why I'm here or a runaway?"

"Nothing, I just thought I'd see if I were right about you," She paused for a moment and erupted, "Yea, I can imagine how you preps are, you can be a runaway too."

Confidently Andrew told her, "It's mid-winter break and I thought I'd get out of the house. I don't live too, too far away."

Resting an arm on the table, and her head on that arm, she asked Andrew, "Okay, then where is home?"

Andrew for a second paused, trying to think of something good to say, but heck, why not be honest, "Port Chester."

"Port Chester? Where in the hell is that." She asked, almost as if she knew already.

"Down in Westchester County, by the state border. You just take route nine about a good fifty miles down and then take 287 east about twelve and you're there." And he said it with great confidence

"You did come a long way," the young lady replied to Andrew, but much more calmly, in fact, she was talking now in a rather shy manner.

Andrew took another bite to finish up his breakfast sandwich. He joked to her, "And you know, the best part is that I do not even have a car and commuted the whole way up here today. At least down here you get good public transportation to pretty much go anywhere without needing a car."

"That's good," the Venus continued as she bounded up suddenly, "And how are you getting home?"

Sipping his coffee, Andrew replied to her, "The same way I came up."

The young lady burst out in another flurry of giggles; Andrew was confused for this chick was rather strange and wild, even though she looked no older than himself. Yet, he kind of liked her, with all that vitality, but you know, there was again the thought of Caroline that would refuse to leave his pathetic little mind. He could not sacrifice his devoted, "love," for this one, no matter how hot.

The beauty suddenly spoke again, "By the way, what's your name?"

"Andrew, Andrew Thomas Stevens," he had no problem at all letting this young lady know his whole name, after all, it would make him but all that more dapper in-front of this love goddess. "What's yours?"
"
Amanda Pfeffer, it means I'm 'spicy' in German," she said with a cheerful vitality. If Nicole was all sweetness, then Amanda was all energy. Suddenly, she made an offer to Andrew, "You want to ride around town with me. It gets kinda boring in the car alone. Come on!"

Surprised and speechless, Andrew did not know what to do now since he was nervous, after all, she seemed aggressive for a stranger and he did not know what to make of it. For all one knows, she might be some crazed psycho killer out to hang his cock on some sort of gory trophy case that shrinks tell us serial killers have. Then again, she's hot, and young, and what the hell, he kind of liked her. "Sure, let's go, I got nothing to do." They both got up and chucked what was left of their little breakfast and went out the door together.

Walking outside the place, Andrew lets the beauty walk in-front of him to her car, a dark blue sixty something muscle car. She tells Andrew in a more sedate tone, "This is my first car and it can haul some ass. Too bad it gets some shitty gas mileage, but what the hell, I think it still looks better than my dad's old lambo."

Andrew, paying more attention to her Ass, just agreed with her, "Yea, I bet." Then it hit him; her had had a Lambo, and jet? "Your dad a lambo too, and Jet? Your family really is rich, and they got you this too!"

"Dad was a CEO and an old fighter pilot, we flew around the world together and got to see many things most people only dream of." She had a proud twinkle in her eye saying that.

"I know the feeling," Andrew added as they continued to make their way to the car.

Bark. Bark, bark, bark, and an even meaner BARK. The two standing only feet away from the car see the wretched dog, the one that chased Andrew, come walking from behind the car, growling and drooling a blood lust. Fire burned in its eyes, and one could see the very devil himself in its attack posture. Amanda for a moment had a concerned look in her face and Andrew was frozen in place, but Amanda wiped the concern off her face and quickly picked up a piece of asphalt from the ground and threw it at the dog, just missing it and forcing it back a bit. Then she picked up another piece of asphalt and threw at the dog, this time hitting it on the forehead. The creature at once turned and scurried away from them. Amanda taunted the thing, "Yea, Bitch, take that you stupid dog!"

Andrew was impressed by her quick thinking and courage and said to her quite candidly, "You are one helluva woman."

"Yea," she said proudly, "I get that alot. I get all solos cause I'm the only one with the balls to take em!"

"I bet," Andrew told her, and then realizing what she had said about solos asked her, "Wait, Solos? Are you a musician?"

"Yep, I play Trumpet," boastfully she told Andrew. "I have had many good teachers over the years."

Andrew, quite surprised, told her, as they approached the car, "I'm a trumpet player too you know. That's my thing."

"Cool beans," she said as she opened the door to the car and Andrew walked around to the passenger side.

Amanda opened the door for Andrew who, climbed on in. On the seat was a sky chart along with many assorted notes, and he asked her, "You're a star gazer too?"

"Yea," she told him, "I like to look at the stars at night. There are just so many of them, and they are in so many different places no matter where you go."

Gently Andrew replied to her, "Yea, I do a lot of star gazing myself. I tend to get a little more technical with things, but I enjoy the beauty and vastness of the night sky."

"I bet," Amanda added, and then turned to him as they both closed the doors, "So how good are you on the trumpet?"

Andrew with the magnificent return of his trademark smirk turned to her and said candidly, "I play the Hayden, Hummel, and

Leopold Mozart trumpet concertos from memory and let us not forget 'Carnival of Venice', Arban style ;)."

Amanda's eyes almost popped out of her head, but had something to say about the last one, "'Carnival of Venice.'"

"Arban Style, madam. Those variations kick ass."

Impressed by the talk, but suspicious of the claims, Amanda stared at Andrew sternly and said, "I know what you are talking about, but how do I know that you're not lying."

"Give me a trumpet, a mouth piece and I'll show you how playing is done."

Amanda smiled and reached to the back seat where low and behold she pulled out a brown trumpet case, quickly, and plopped it down on Andrew's lap. "Play," she confidently told Andrew, folding her arms and plastering a smile on her face.

Quickly, Andrew open up the case to reveal an expensive silver plated but dinged up horn and said a few words as he looked for the mouthpiece to play with, "You know, I have been playing for damn well nine years now, and all those years I kicked ass. I'm sorry, but it is my job to be good, you know." Andrew found the mouthpiece and put the horn together now and turned to Amanda and said, "Now this is how one kicks ass with a trumpet." With flash and brilliance Andrew begins to play beginning to the Arban's variations on that old favorite mentioned before. It starts out rather slow and boring, and Amanda was delighted by his tone and prefect phrasing, but it did not sound so tough. Then, suddenly Andrew pauses and goes into a wild flurry of playing like a madman. Notes are flying all over the place and obvious by the sound the virtuoso technical demands are meet and all Amanda could do was gawk at Andrew's playing. He only played a short section, but it was enough to leave her speechless.

She said to him, humbled, "God damn, you're good."

With the ever-famous smirk on his face, Andrew told her, "I have a bad habit of being good." There was pause, and Andrew spoke out, "So, are we rolling," as he put the horn away.

Amanda with a wicked smile on her face said, "Sure, we'll get rolling. Just hurry up putting that thing away."

Andrew complied and finished putting it way and tossed it in the back. Amanda just quietly put the car in reverse, it was stick to his amazement, backed away from the parking spot and reminded Andrew, "Put on those seat belts cause it's gonna be a bumpy ride."

She slammed on the accelerator and they were off.

"You're fucking insane," Andrew yelled as next thing one knows, Amanda is driving through the streets of this town and through the residential neighborhoods in the morning at lightning speed. Andrew had some more to complain loudly, "You are going to get us killed." Andrew watched the needle almost hit ninety.

"Ah, come on! Have some fun!", Amanda replied to Andrew as suddenly she braked the car at a down sloping intersection, "Shit, cop!"

"At our six," Andrew asked her, half mortified.

"No, at eleven heading two," Amanda noted to Andrew who saw a police car casually drive away before them up another street. Amanda also had a comment for Andrew, "Why are you so scared. Life sucks, so make it better. I just want to enjoy whatever is left in it."

Calmer, being that they were not moving, Andrew looked into himself, and wondered why is it that he is so concerned about life or death. Had he not just held a gun to his own head hours ago? He had to be honest, "I don't know. It just feels wrong to end my life now. It feels like I have so much more to do, but I also don't want to live in this world anymore."

Amanda turned to look at him and peacefully asked, "Do you believe in God?"

"Sometimes."

"Why?"

Turning to Amanda, and looking straight into her powerful blue eyes, "Cause then all this shit called life seems worth living, worth suffering, when I believe."

Quieter, Amanda looked ahead a little and drove down the street slowly to a group of stores going up a hill to a residential neighborhood. She pulled over calmly and said, "Maybe you should get off here. We're both people who need time alone. I just spend the weekend cleaning up my daddy's brains off the marble, and I still don't understand why anybody would want to kill him. I guess that's why I drove." Her face had turned almost an ashen gray, too sad for even tears.

Andrew starred for a moment at her conceptualizing what she just uttered and the look on her face. She was beyond devastated. He asked, "Your dad is dead?"

She just stared ahead and said without looking at him, "someone robbed the house and blew his brains out. I haven't stopped driving." She was biting down on her lips, her face vacillating between tears and anger. "They haven't found the bastards, but I will." She shook her head and repaired her demeanor, "daddy raised me to be a strong one, so I will be."

Andrew turned to look out at the stores they were next now, and turned back to look at Amanda one last time as he opened the door. "You know, you are one crazy, wacky, and wild Woman, meaning, simply the coolest. I hope you find whoever killed your father. I guess we say bye here."

"Yep," she quickly as she looked down the road, "We'll see each other again."

"Yea, I hope so, good luck Amanda," Andrew told her as he stepped out of the car and closed the door. "Look me up sometime, I go to Stepinac," He yelled out loud so she could hear him through the glass. She let out a big grin and at that they waved each other goodbye, Amanda sprinted away in her car with the deep throaty roar of the car's pushrod V8 trailing in her wake.

Andrew stood there, looking at this fireball of a woman disappear, thinking what he could do if he had that kind of vitality, that zest, that ability to just bounce back from tragedy, and drive a nice car.

It had begun to cloud up a bit, like there was another flurry ready to come through. Looking up to the skies, Andrew came to miss Amanda already. Perhaps there was more to say, perhaps there was more to know about this young lady that has passed by like a summer breeze, in winter. Andrew started walking, and seeing no one around on this dull morning, he thought out loud to himself. "What a strange and wild one she is, and to think that perhaps I'll never see her again. It just suits me right. Just little more than a year ago I accepted my lonely lot, but now I'm chasing Caroline, and have strangers tugging at my heart too. What a freaking joke life is. Why do choices have to be so damned hard.

## Chapter 6: The Atheist Priest.

He continued walking up the street and saw it bend around a corner up to the right on a small hill. He walked on leisurely and took note of the quiet residential neighborhood he was in. Lots of trees seemed to line the road, keeping a solemn watch on all those who passed by. He developed a glum look on his face, a frightened confusion. One end was checked by a painful life and evil dog, while the other went on into the unknown. The skies grew darker and the smell of snow wandered into his nostrils. As he walked further up the hill, Andrew spotted a church up ahead. It was a simple red brick affair, nothing like the grand churches he was accustomed to across the river. However, though, it was not a feeling of nostalgia or comfort in bosom from an unseen god that was boiling up inside of him, no, it was something different. He felt inside of him a burning anger, a betrayal, and bitterness that drew him close to this church. He firmly walked up to the brown wooden doors and threw them open.

Sternly and with the severest of looks on his face, Andrew marched up to the very front of the church and looked upon the alter. He took only quick note of the barren alter and white interior, free of any decoration. He knelt down on the pew, took off his hat and looked up to the altar, clutching his hat tightly in his hands. His eyes began to water and he protested to the heavens.

"Are you for real Lord? Are you! This is my dark exile; this is my pain. Life is a two-faced thing. The sight of friends and places oh so near and dear to me colored my canvas. Textured by all the little everyday adventures that marked my life. It was beautiful, but only for a precious little while, for now it has all turned on me. Yes, this evil bitch, this cunt, this evil life! I am in pain because of it! I have been made into nothing, nothing! I have been made to fail my promise to myself, my friends and you my God, if you're for real. I don't know what to think anymore. All that my hands touch turn to dust and all that I long for vanishes into the night. All these sixteen years have been frittered away by the pestilence known as life! I deserve better! Look at me, I'm a good boy! I help people, I do my religious duties, and hell, while I am at it I kept my fucking fly up! Where the fuck are you God!

"Where's victory and success for all my toil? Where is that little bit of happiness that I can touch with my hands, see with my eyes and taste with my mouth? Why do the assholes of this world get more than me, and I don't just mean the material Lord?

"Most of my friends have left me, and an outcast I have become. And I will lose them all when I finally become an orphan, not that I'm already since the dawn of my memories, in case you haven't noticed. Where is the money to support my habit, my school, my home! And all my musical achievements have been forgotten in favor of my botched up schedule and new instructors who envy me, hate me, and have suppressed me. Then there is her, the one girl I love who remains too elusive for me to even dare love. Look at how good I have been about the ladies; where is my recompense? I am obsessed, obsessed by that longing for, 'what should have been.' She should have been mine, and the first chair in band as well. My eyes tear from the moments that never were but should have been. I cry cause of all those friends who left me because of a stupid lie. I look at my empty shelves and want for the un-fated trophies and awards to appear to justify my hope, but none appear. I was born into a suck ass team who could never win a game even if their lives depended on it! I dread what will be. I dread the loneliness that I have never gotten used to. I am nerd, a misfit, a thinker of another kind; I am a reject because of it all! Every passing day there is a singing soprano, a siren from across the ways beckoning me to go ahead and pull the trigger and spray the walls with my 'brillant,' brain, but not even death will have me, now that I want her so bad. All that I want, all that I need I can't have, and that which I get, I hate!

"Hope, where are you? Once we were like lovers, married and united as one. Once before the ramparts of life together would we conquer the armies of fate! Well, that was before, and this is my now. Lonely now, and alone, and misery is my lot Lord. I am a miserable shade! Human, all too human! How I wish I were something else, something better so I could rise above this pain. I must look up to see the tiniest of worms; even the ants tower over me. I am now less than nothing; I am a negative. Hear me oh God if you are for real and admonish me for this sin! I dare you! Lay upon me my dire demise! I dare you! Such has been my crimes of failure! I dare you! I am suffering too terribly from the terminal disease, life!

"This is the end of my paved road. What lies beyond is up to my hated enemy chance, by whom I have been captured and raped; by whom I have been made pregnant with bastard mediocrity, only giving birth to more pain like an eternal Ouroboros of suck. I am nothing but a stupid hairless gorilla like the rest of mankind, a meaningless meatbag! I hate me, I hate me, I very much hate me! I hate this life! I am way past my wits end! I can't! I can't be happy being human if this is what it means! I have to be better to be happy, I have to be above pain. Am I so wrong, or am I right? I can't live up to life itself, and so then, what can I live up to. The answer is nothing. If I cannot live then I must die, but even at that I have failed. I have not stored up the grace for a happy death, and I am all too unworthy of the privilege it seems, even though I am just an innocent boy! I suffer, but not even death will have anything to do with me. Are you content with my suffering yet, you fucking sadist!"

"Into the valley of darkness, exiled from Eden. An innocent exile have I become, even in my dreams, and forever it seems shall my pathetic little soul be tortured by, "what if," and, "what should have been." What can free me? What can take me to the promise land out of this Egypt? Farewell happiness, farewell my love, oh dear blessed hope, huh? All I wanted was someone to love, someone to hold, and be happy with like everybody else in absence of everything else, but that's probably just hormones talking. I want to be worth something; to matter and be important. I have to know that I was somebody, but I don't see that. I see in the eyes of all people the meaninglessness of life. Where are you my God this day? Where is the proof? Did you not hear a damned thing I said! I want a better life! I want a real life! I want a good life! I want to be happy and content for once! I WANT TO LOVE YOU AGAIN! Give me a reason Lord! That is all. Is that, too much, to ask for?"

A pause, and a sinister, old voice form behind said, "Yes.......it is."

Andrew turned to see who it was from the back that spoke. He stood up from the pew and saw in back of church, sitting in a wheel chair, a wrinkled old man in a priest's collar. Andrew, too bitter to be friendly to the intruder, questioned him, "Who are you? Have you been listing to me this whole time?"

"I am a quiet one," the mysterious priest replied as his eyes rolled around like that of a madman. "I like to sneak up on the unsuspecting people and listen to their pleas and supplications to the great unseen God."

Andrew walked out from the pew and began walking back towards this priest, and inquisitively looking at him, this odd breed of clergy before him. His appearance was frazzled, his hygiene looked unkempt, and he was dribbling from the side of his mouth, yet strangely he was able to articulate quite well, in a rather cynical way. Andrew sat down again two pews from him and began to interrogate him, "Are you some reject from a nursing home psych ward?"

The odd priest turned to look at Andrew and replied to him in a more normal manner, "Hardly. I am but an ornament to this church; a broken relic. I don't believe in anything, but that everything is, well, absurd."

Andrew's eyes opened wide in surprise for here he was hearing a priest talk like this. Surely the man was mad, but still, it caught him off guard. Curious though, he inquired further, "you are a priest. How can you not believe in a God?"

"I cannot believe what I cannot see, and what I see I cannot believe. I don't see anything but little details, wheels attached to axles, heads on bodies, and planters with fake trees. Where is the God of the weak and miserable? 'I don't see you.' Maybe he went on vacation, a long, long vacation, but, I have yet to see him."

"How did you become priest," Andrew inquired.

The priest took a good hard look at Andrew and with his round bug eyes told him, "Once I was a young boy like you and I believed whatever was feed to this bag of meat and poo while strapped to my societal high chair like a helpless little infant. Once I could accept anything, and every pain I could explain away, and so I believed, so much so in fact that I devoted my life to him," he said pointing to the alter with his withered hand. He continued, "I spent fifty years preaching of the absurd, and proclaiming the absurd, till one day I could no more. Eighty years and I have seen nothing, heard nothing, or felt nothing, other than the clothes on my back and the creaking of my old age! So now from this chair I look back on the life that should have been, and the fun that I could have had, but alas, I was a high priest for the mediocre and such is my reward. I get to dribble all day and masticate over what should have been. Do yourself a favor boy, and end it now before your life becomes nothing more than an empty shell of what it is already."

This took Andrew aback. This priest had to be a madman, a senile waif in a wheelchair, but it was sensible in only the most ghastly way. Andrew stood up and began to step back from him as the madman, this atheist priest as he began singing, "Faith of our fathers living still, in spite of dungeon, fire and sword. Oh how our hearts beat out with joy, whenever we hear his glorious word. Faith of our fathers living still we will be true to thee till death."

Andrew, without saying a word, stepped around him and quietly fled that church

## Chapter 7:  The Savage Frontier.

Back into the light, the light of day, outside now from the darkened catacomb that was seemingly that church he had left behind, Andrew wandered on, pulled by some inner force further west, out into the country now. With every slow, hard, ponderous step Andrew took, the world faded till all the sounds of civilization, the cars, people, streets, and town vanished away like ghosts. Every step loosed its thunder, and the cold wind died down to a calm breeze. Soon all he could hear was the sound of his own heart beating, that desperate sound of the torture he was in. It was quiet, and devoid of life, one almost expects tumbleweed to go rolling by. The spot from where he stood had an expansive view of the sky. It was gray now and looked so very big, frighteningly huge like a beast poised to swallow. Behind him lay a seemingly broken life, and scary people, but also a narrow, sparkling trail of cherished memories, but only that, memories. Ahead of him is the unknown. Pain or triumph, that is what lies ahead of every future, and none know which. He could go back now or he can go forward to see what is ahead in the unknown. With a forward step, he chose to pressed on.

He began to walk very severely down the road, marching almost to the rhythmic drum beating of his heart. He was going someplace to find an answer to his problem, life. He looked ahead with the most marshal of expressions; he walked on like this until he came upon a parking lot to the left and just beyond it an opening into some woods. He could read a sign by the opening that declared this a nature trail. He was curious as to where it would take him. He crossed the street and walked over diligently, marching in like a solider. He walked into this trail that was surrounded by two gray, ominous rock outcroppings. It was like walking into the jaws of a beast. He was compelled to go in, a tugging in his chest pulled him towards this maw. Entering, he saw a shadow descended over the land. Clouds were moving in quickly, rapidly it seemed oscillating between light and dark as they teased the sun overhead, intermittently blocking it. He stopped, and shuttered a moment. A

71

cold wind blew and he could smell the approach of snow again. He grew nervous because he had no shelter but only the clothes on his back. He did not relish freezing to death, but he had also heard that hypothermia might also be a painless death, under the right conditions. It would also be an embarrassing demise. He could turn around and go back to civilization, but what good would that do him, other than of course keep him warm and alive another day in misery, a prisoner in his own life. He could go on and see what tomorrow might bring, back to the gun, or the beast and be consumed whole and defecated out only to be consumed again by the worms in the ground. He could go back to all his problems on the other side of the river and slowly rot from them like a tree stump. It would be the easy thing, after all, he can do himself in from another bout of misery or he can let this infernal winter do him in tonight. It is so easy to die, but so hard to survive, let alone live.

Looking ahead and feeling the first snowflake fall on his face he was ready to take an about face and go back, but he heard something. He heard a strange whispering sound ahead of him, like that of someone speaking in the distance. He was captivated by it; perhaps there was somebody interesting to talk to ahead, and perhaps there was some sort of shelter, an answer, and that's when

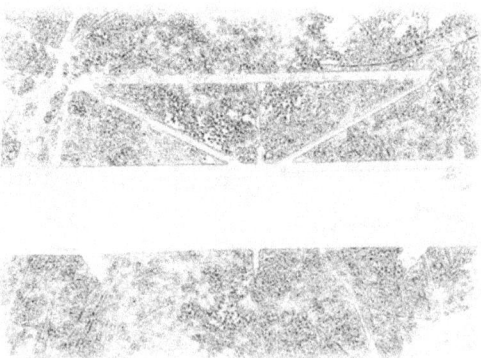

he heard another sound, one more ominous and sinister from behind. He heard the familiar distant barking of that dog. Now Andrew's leg began to move, faster into these woods of uncertainty.

Two hours must have past, and Andrew grew tired and weary. This trail he had walked into was indeed a nature trail, but a long one. He must have been hearing things when he heard the whispers in the woods. Perhaps the wind and his lonely mind were playing tricks on him. Needless to say, he was due for a break. In these lightly snow-covered woods, he found a large round rock to sit upon. He walked up to it and took a seat, feeling the coldness of the rock creep up his back. Andrew kept his ears ever vigilant for the sound of that hellhound, the one that would not leave him alone. He looked back to where he had come from to see if he spotted the foul beast, but he could see nothing other than the ghostly wisps of snow blowing in the breeze. He looked intently in that direction, almost expecting the foul beast to appear. He was apprehensive and worried. No rabid dog could be so pathological as this beast; no rabid beast could be so persistent. It has no collar, or tags, no signs on it that it had belonged to anyone. It was simply that, an evil nightmare, supernatural in its countenance, and following him.

On the rock, Andrew was startled suddenly by the rush of leaves. He turned to look at the other directions and saw a backpacker approaching. He had a pair of blue jeans on and an orange coat on with patches of brown on the chest and arms. He also had a large red backpack on rails that looked heavy, but probably wasn't. Andrew studied this man approaching. He was older with a large graying beard. He had glasses and he could see clearly that he had a gray wool cap on. The old man looked up himself to see the stranger ahead of him. He called out to the boy, "You are a strange sight to see?"

Andrew, hearing his gruff voice answered him politely, "I'm not sure what you mean?"

The old man stopped in front of Andrew, stripping off his backpack and laying it down, began to explain to him, "I find it very strange to find a well-dressed young man such as yourself this far up the trail."

Andrew did not know quite what to tell him since he scarcely knew what he was doing there himself. He told him quite simply, "I am just getting some air. I've had a rough day and thought I would take a walk."

The old man asked Andrew, "So where did you park?"

Andrew did not want to get into too long a conversation with the old man because he felt a bit uncomfortable, so he told him, "well, I parked at the entrance of this trail. I've walked all the way since."

The old man looked intently at the boy and inquired him about his age, "You look a little young. Are you one of the college students around here?"

Andrew told him in a confidant manner that belied his current inner turmoil, "Oh yea, I go to New Paltz."

"Really," The old man exclaimed. "I used to teach there but now I teach across the water at Marist. So how do you like it over there?"

Andrew was not sure what to say since he never so much as set foot in the town. He said quite simply, "Oh, it's quiet, for me that is."

The old man doubted that and told him, "Quiet! Last time I checked it was still quite the party school."

Embarrassed, Andrew told him, "Well, not compared to other schools in the state."

"That is certainly true," the old man told Andrew, very entertained. He continued on, "You know, now that I think about it, When I was younger I used to dress like that. In fact, later on in life, when I was in the military for while I had a Coat almost exactly like that."

Carrying on the conversation that looked to ward off the lonely boredom he was feeling, Andrew added, "Yea, actually this is a military coat. This belonged to my father, he was in the Air Force."

"Well, that's good," the old man told him, "Yea, I was a Marine myself. My dad made me join, it was family tradition. It was during Nam, but I was lucky I didn't go there. I had a cushy desk job as a journalist. I covered all the cocktail parties in Washington."

Andrew smiled a bit and asked him, "That was interesting, did you feel glad to not have to fight?"

"I'm glad I'm alive, a lot of people I knew did not survive. Kinda feel guilty about it sometimes, but the war was unjust anyway and evil. I'm glad I was not a part of it. I just wrote my articles and had my fun with the ladies." They both began to laugh. The Old man, regaining his composers asked Andrew, "So, what did your dad do?"

Trying to match that humor, Andrew replied, "he spends his time being shot at those years."

"Oh," The old man said with a concerned look on his face, "I see, that is tough. What exactly did he do?"

"He flew F-4Cs and Es."

The old man stood back a moment and nodded in a respectful way. He asked, "What's his name?"

"Thomas Stevens."

"Thomas Stevens, of Port Chester?" the old man asked with an excited look on his face.

"Yep, that's him."

"Oh my goodness, no wonder you caught my eye. You look

just like your father. Yes, yes, I remember now. We did some work together in the seventies down in Washington. I remember I was working for this lobbying group and your dad came over from his to work on behalf of the auto industry to fight the CAFE standards."

Andrew was bewildered by what he was talking about and inquired further, "You worked with him? He has not told me much about his time after the Air Force."

"Well, I only remember him for that one project. He got in a bit of a scandal thought in the days before Iran Contra, and it would have much bigger if it was not for that. I heard he got into a really bad accident."

A bitterness was awoken in Andrew as he knew all too well about that part of his life. "Yes, he did have a bad accident. Things were very different afterwards."

"I see." At that moment the old man lifted his arm and pulled back his sleeve to reveal his wristwatch. He took a glance at it and bid his farewell to Andrew. "Well, I got to keep walking. Good meeting you young man. See if your father can remember me."

"I'll see if he can, so long," Andrew replied as he watched the old man continue on his way. Andrew thought about how odd the situation was, but he brushed it aside. He got up and continued on his way forward towards the unknown. More pointedly he said to himself, "I can't escape my life no matter where I go."

About half an hour later, the woods had become more menacing and the skies were growing ever darker. Evening was beginning to drop its dark veil and a great anxiety began to tear into the heart and soul of Andrew. The trail had become rough and more primitive. For all he knew he could have just wandered off it and not known it for the snow hid much of the ground below. The cold began to penetrate his clothes and he was becoming desperate for some comfort, not so much his survival. His steps had become slow and lethargic; he needed his rest. The questions of, "whether I should live or not," began to turn into questions of, "how do I warm up?" Then, like an evil shrike meant to kill his soul, he heard a distant cry of a screaming man and the menacing bark of that hellhound. Andrew filled up with fear.

He began running, running faster into the woods, further and deeper, scared and desperate. If he wanted to die, it was not like this, in pain, mauled to death by a menacing dog from the very pit of hell. His weary legs became light like feathers and his adrenalin surged through his body like a cascade, fueling him to run and run faster and faster. His energy was up and in the back of his head he could hear the tearing of flesh, and the smell of his own blood and torn bowels. He kept running and kept running till his legs became heavy and lungs began to burn. He kept running, but soon his flight became a jog. He kept running till his jog became a walk. He kept running until all stopped and he fell.

There he was like a shattered man on a hard pillow of snow and rotten leaves. He lay there face down, exhausted and breathing heavily. His eyes closed and between breaths he begged, "I don't', I don't, I, I don't want, to be torn, to pieces." So, like a wicked beast of darkness, the night fell. It was dark, and Andrew turned like a rat-infested corpse and looked to the sky above. Only a dark blue hue shown. Clouds covered a good portion of the sky and soon there would be complete and total darkness. Even the adjusted eyes of Andrew could hardly peer into the woods surrounding, and it would not be surprising at all if he fell of a cliff amongst these bluffs and hills, because looking about in what little light was left, he had unknowingly run up a hill. Fear was his only companion now and all it whispered into his ear was death. He was seeing how ugly it really was, and at least for the moment wanted nothing to do with it. He picked himself up, wondering if it was best to just stop where he was and sleep on the spot, but soon the sound of rustling branches and the cold biting wind remind him that he has to find some sort of shelter to live into the morning light.

His feet were now cold and getting more numb by the

minute.  Rather than utterly fall into a blind panic, he chose to be appropriately concerned and nothing more.  So, pulling out from his pocket a small key chain flashlight, he squeezed the sides and thanks to the ghostly reflectivity of the snow he could see all around his person.  He began to look around and spotted right below him a wall of rock and vegetation.  He jumped down before and realized what it was good for.  He could build a fire across the way and have these rocks reflect the heat back towards him.  It was a clever ploy, but one he had learned from his many youthful adventures with his father's friends.  He took off his gloves dug into his trusty pocket and pulled out his good old pocketknife.  Onward he proceeded to pull out the knife blade and set it down in the ground while he puts his gloves back on.  He had to build a fire and fuel it with something.  But there was also something else.

With his little flashlight, Andrew went about looking, scouring for a smooth stone or something to use as a flint.  He overturned a nearby branch and found his stone.  Next he looked about for some small branches and picked up all that he could.  He cleared a patch of leaves with his shoe and placed branches there and some dried leaves that were clinging to the branch.  He began striking the stone with the blade from his knife and watch the sparks fly.  He did this repeatedly for a good fifteen minutes before he saw a small flame, a light, erupt in the darkness.  He knelt down and began to blow on it, its life giving breath.  The flame grew and grew till soon it began to consume the whole pile.  Andrew stood back and marveled at the fire, at the light.  How good the smell of burning wood was at this moment, like a warm stove.  With the light from the small fire now, he was able to look about and find more twigs and small branches to throw on the flame to grow it and keep it burning.  He looked at his fire and saw that it was good.  This was the first hour.

The hour passed by rather quickly as he looked about for more tinder, pumping more wood into the fire to keep it burning and make it larger.  He also remembered to create a nice ring of stones to contain his fire, so it would not spread too far.  He went to sit down between the fire and the wall and could feel warmth radiating to the spot in-between. Getting up, he walked around again, looking for a good log or two to throw in so that he could have something that would burn long through the night while he slept. He happened around his lit space upon three rather heavy and large logs broken off from rot off a larger one, most likely maple, a good long burning wood. They were heavy, about a good ten or fifteen pounds each, but seemingly water logged, yet when he put the first on in the fire, he could see it start to burn well, and more importantly, slowly. It was a comfort and he again went to sit in his space. He curled up into a ball and began to fall asleep, warmed in the soothing comfort of his fire. Andrew was so proud of this little achievement.

He awoke, shivers going down his spine. His eyes peeled open and he saw his fire waning. Quickly he looked at his watch and noticed two hours had passed. There was not much left of his fire, just glowing coals. He lurched out of his space and began piling on leaves in an effort to revive it, and it mildly worked. As the flames slowly grew again, he threw in some of the twigs and other assorted wood he had previously collected. Once the fire was roaring again, he threw in his second log, larger than the first. He curled himself back into a ball and looked down at his flames again, pondering his creation once more before sleep overtook him again.

A loud crackle, and he awoke. Panicked, and concerned he got up and began to look around furiously. Again, he looked at his watch and saw that this time he managed three hours of sleep. He scanned around and peered into the darkness to see if there were any malevolent shadows, but none appeared. "It was probably just the fire," he thought to himself, but as before, though, his fire was now just hot glowing coals. So, he threw in more tinder and sought to grow the fire again, which like before he had a great deal of success. Finally, with the fire renewed, he threw in his last log, knowing, of course, that once that log was exhausted he would have to get up and move on.

His fire was burning brightly, but there was crackling, but in the background. Suddenly fear filed into his being, and his nerves began shake. He looked around frantically in the dark and pulled out his pocketknife. From the black he heard an angry groaning knew that this had to be his challenger, this Dog had found him in the night. There was a long pointy stick next to him on the ground and Andrew cautiously picked it up and armed himself with, like a spear of old. Finding it too small and useless for this battle, he cautiously closed his pocketknife and put it away. Ahead of him, out of the shadows emerged ever so menacingly the black dog, that all too familiar beast that chased him before. It's figure seemingly glowing a dark scarlet from the flickering light of the fire and its black coat. They stared at each other looking into each other's glassy eyes. Slowly it seemed that they did their slow dance of death round the fire, each getting more agitated, more ready to fight. Andrew lost all fear now, and he was shaking not from fright, but anger, hate, and fight. Suddenly they reached a point where there was no fire between them and now there was do or die, now was the fight, now they did battle and beast ran at the boy leaping for his neck. Andrew with his wooden rod at his right hand turned swiftly and gored the side of the beast as it brushed up against his chest. It kicked wildly and thrashed them to the ground together. Andrew pushed upon stick to dig it in and violently kicked the animal, and kicked, harder and harder till he heard bones breaking and body became tender. He felt no more struggle. It's heavy breaths rapidly slowed to quiet stillness. It was dead.

He stepped back and looked down at the beast, it did not move. Its blood he could plainly see in the firelight oozing from the wound inflicted by his weapon, yet none of it miraculously on his person or hands. Andrew was numb, he stood like a statue staring at this site, at this work of his. Never in his life did he violently kill a creature like this before. Never before in his life did he have to protect himself from death like this. Violence, it was something he would talk about, joke about, something he would watch, but does even an old school fight lead to things such as this? How different felling a deer or lion is from a distance than killing it practically with your bare hands. This was new, this was graphic, this was horrifying, but his only other choice was mutilation in the night. With a sudden, inexplicable furry, he grabbed the creature by the hind legs and dragged it into the fire to watch it burn, to turn to ashes, to vanish from his mind and make sure that it would never come back ever again. His holocaust to survival. This was his choice, for this bringer of death to burn in the dark of night.

Morning and the snow glisten in the light. The trees stood straight and tall, motionless in this morning. The sky was clear and blue with only a few birds flying about looking for some road kill. Heavy, and slow, Andrew's eyes opened and he glared out before him. He had slept the remainder of the night seated before the warming fire. He peered out before him at the coals of his old fire and the grotesque sight of a cremated monster. It was roasted thoroughly to ash in places and whatever else was not dust let out a sweet smell of barbequed meat. Of course, hungry though he was, Andrew was not going to eat the creature, in fact, he was disgusted at the sight; the drippings of fat that began run through the rocks and down the hill a little. Becoming now more alert, the boy got up and stretched. He took one more look at the place where he had built his life-giving fire and roasted the beast. He turned away and never looked back.

With the light of morning, he could see that from here it was all downhill to a dirt road below. It was surprising that through the course of the night one had not so much as seen the light of a passing car, or that nobody noticed the fire, but then again it was perhaps nothing more than a private or closed road of sorts. It did not matter much though, it was a destination, and so the boy climbed down.

The way down was difficult and perilous, several times did Andrew almost take a tumble, but always he managed to stay on his feet. He kept his pace and descended in only a quarter hour a considerable distance; after all, these hills are rather large. Once he reached the road, he found it to be nothing more than a kind of path made up of gravel and broken up stones. The wind and sun took care of blowing away the top layer of snow and raggedly exposing the surface below. It was doubtful that this was the kind of road that traffic would be on. He looked both ways to see which way he wanted to go, and elected to go right, north more as seemingly there was this pull inside of him to move further and further away from, "home." Walking down this road he looked ahead him towards the distance and noticed a black object on the side of the road. It looked vaguely like a car, but he was not too sure, so he started walking faster and faster till he found himself running. After about a minute or two of running he approached it. Looking closely at it, he saw that it was an older black hatchback that looked like it was pulled over for some reason or another. Slowly he walked up to it and studied it closely. He saw the doors partially opened and the hatchback open with the contents of a duffel bag strewn about the back. He walked over to them and investigated them. He saw that they were gym like materials like sports tape, compress, and shorts. They seemed to belong to a woman. Peering now inside the car, he looked down at the gray seats and in the front on the driver's side door and dash he saw blood. The pool of blood inside was frozen. It was sprayed on the dash, floor and seat. It has been a messy death. Shattered glass was also present on the inside seats, glistening in the light. He leapt back and frantically started looking around. The hard-frozen ground revealed no tracks. If anything, his best bet was to keep heading straight to where the car might have come from and see if he could get the authorities. Quickly he scampered off.

It was a challenge to make it through this tertiary road of sorts, the ground was so broken up, it was hard to see how the car even got that far accidently. On either side of him, there were large hills that loomed over him like unfriendly giants, waiting for their chance to smite him. He kept his pace, holding a rather concerned look on his face. He was edgy right now, not knowing if it was a crime scene or accident of sorts. It bothered him that from these hills there could be a killer or other associated psycho watching over him like a predator, and certainly he was an easy target being the only living soul on that road right now, holding the low ground and armed only with a small pocket knife. "Don't bring a pocket knife to a gunfight," he mused to himself. Still, he had to press on, his body was numb to pain and tiredness right now, there was only this mission now to find somebody and let them know what he saw. He kept moving and almost tripped on something, he looked down and saw the barrel portion of a destroyed break action shotgun. There was also evidence but body, but hey, at least gun to be pointed his way either. Finally, Andrew got to the end of this road where there was a fence and red farmhouse, looking empty and abandoned. However, on the other side of that fence was a real road, plowed, salted and clean; its wet pavement shimmering in the rising morning sun. On the approached he saw a police car go by in its blue and gold, but it vanished away round a bend. Still, he had reached somewhere where he could be seen. As he reached the edge of this path, he squeezed his way through the fence and was on the road to civilization.

## Chapter 8: The Trojan Horse

There was more walking to do, and more thinking to do. He had hoped that civilization, or at least a place to eat would be nearby, but after an exhausting hour of pedestrian drudgery, he was far away. He had made it to a long straight road that was pretty busy this morning. It was like all things on this journey, half comforting and half annoying that yes, he was nearing some sort of civilization based on how busy the road was, but also disconcerting by how long it was, and seemingly leading nowhere. Finally, he got a scent. Coffee and pancakes filled the air and he could see to his left cropping up what looked like the outline of an establishment. An odd mix of luxury cars and well-worn pickup trucks mingled together on the parking lot. Andrew diligently walked across the pavement eager for some sustenance while brushing off his coat and pants the accumulated dust and dirt from the night. He reached the building and pulled open the glass front door. Entering inside there was the thick odor of bacon, eggs, and coffee. Ahead was counter with two cash registers, and to the right the diner portion, and it was here that Andrew's attention was turned. Inside, a giant counter stretched the length of the room, seemingly, with various folks, mostly old men in plaid clothes or denim jackets, sitting on the short round stools down the length of the counter. Across it were some more tables with folks seated in those as well. Obviously, there was the kitchen behind the counter with several women in blue aprons running around attending to all the diners having their breakfast.

Andrew stepped into the dining room and heard from behind the counter one of the waitresses, and old fat woman with her dirty blonde hair captive in a hair net, "I'll be over there to help you sir, just pick a seat." The boy just gave a sincere smile and looked around for a good space to have a seat. The smell of Bacon and eggs did a good job of removing from his mind what he had just seen, if only temporarily, the abandoned car, along with his desperate cold and fatigue. He scanned around a bit like a bird of prey, trying to find a seat and suddenly was seized with surprise at a harsh, yet young female voice that called from right next to him.

"Andrew is it, Brian's friend."

Andrew turned and looked down at the table right next to him and saw a rather disheveled blonde with a very familiar countenance. Still this person could not easily be recognized through her rather messy appearance, a dirty brown coat, frazzled hair and dirt on her face, like someone who just came from a disaster area. "Yea, I know you, you look so familiar."

"Caroline, Nisoyen, I hang out with Brian and his friends sometimes."

There was this electric surge of surprise and shock in him. His spine tingled with a great discomfort, but yes, indeed, this was her, his crush seated here, but still, it did not feel like her, not at least as he remembered her. It was like staring at a stranger. Andrew spoke up and sat down, "Yea, yes, I'm so sorry I didn't recognize you, but you look like..."

"Hell, I know," she put to him quite candidly. She did not have a very friendly look on her face, and her gaze was rather dismissive. This was definitely not how Andrew remembered her, like an angel. She continued on, "I know I look like hell and believe me, I don't enjoy it. Why are you here?"

Still wide eyed in surprise, Andrew sheepishly answered her piercing interrogation, "Well, I got the week off from school so I thought I'd just go round and check some places out. Brian, the guys and I have plans to go camping round here later this year."

Boring into Andrew's eyes with her own, Caroline continued her questioning, "Why are you here, all the way over here at this diner here and now."

"I was just wandering around."

"Liar, tell me why are you out here?"

"I told you I was just wandering around. Look, I saw something on the road and need to call the cops......"

"Tell the truth!"

"I am telling you the truth, I was just wandering around here. I am not here on purpose, stalking you or anything! What the hell are you even doing here?"

Andrew had had to raise his voice and all became silent. Finally, for the first time in more than a day there was whispering, finally he was not the only person in a room, but the center of attention. The old people in the background were talking amongst themselves. Indeed, the waitress that welcomed Andrew in was talking with another old redheaded co-worker about him. Andrew just stared indignantly now at Caroline. It was not so much that he was worried about blowing any chance he would have of dating her, but it was more about his pride. Suddenly she was not the goal, but an aggravation. She was embarrassing him here in public, and he did nothing wrong. "I am not stalking you or anything like I am sure a lot of guys do to you, I am just wandering around here getting to know this area cause I have nothing better to do today, besides, I need to call the cops I saw something."

Her face changed, and suddenly she was smiling and almost laughing. She started to giggle a little and pronounced to him, "You're such a pussy. I could make you blather so easy."

Andrew was confused, and adding to the confusion the waitress finally came over with her little order slip in hand, "Sir, is there anything I can get you?"

"Coffee, milk and sugar, and how about scrambled eggs and toast."

"Just like the lady," the waitress said as she smiled a little and walked away. Andrew was shocked a little, of course, that Caroline had ordered the same thing.

"Yes, appears we like breakfast the same way."

Caroline seemed to be getting into better spirits, and this was very pleasing to Andrew. It certainly helped that they had a little something in common this morning. He added, "So, It's a coincidence that we ordered the same thing, isn't it?"

"It happens."

"So what are you doing up here?"

"I am keeping myself very busy. I had a fencing tourney up at the college here this weekend and I was supposed to come home Sunday night, but my sperm donor's car died. Tried fixing it but I don't know nothing bout cars." She gesticulated alluding to the filth she was covered in.

"So, that would explain a lot. Why are you still stuck here?" Andrew was confused.

Caroline gave Andrew a wicked look and told him, "It's tough when your dad is busy with other things. It so happens he has drill this week. That's why I had to take the car and go by myself."

There was something strange about her explanation. It was not what he recalled her uncle implying. He didn't want to press it too much so he continued on about the breakdown, "So what happened to the truck? When did it die?"

"Sunday night."

"What have you been doing up here since then. It's Tuesday now?"

She smiled again and told him in a rather friendly manner, "Well, I have friends and family up here and I stayed with them. They go to college here at New Paltz. I look like hell, rough night. Had lots of shit to do."

Twisting his face as something did not add up, "Ouch, well

that sucks, how do you plan on getting home?"

"Simple, you'll take me home in your car. How's that."

Andrew was a little embarrassed because he had no car, let alone a driver's license yet. Honestly, he had to tell her since there was no way to hide it, "I didn't come by car. I just kinda sort of rode up here and hoofed it part of the way."

Caroline again had a rather indignant look on her face for a moment, but the red blush suddenly vanished and she seemed to put a smile on her face, "Okay, that's alright. I'm sure you just turned sixteen. Hell, I just got my license only in December. You do have some money or something so we can get back home, right?"

"Hell yea," Andrew assuredly told her, "I got enough for both us and then some. Hell, I got a hundred bucks on me. I could take us both to Albany right now if I wanted to."

"Well good, good, that's very good. At least we won't have to be stuck here. I only have enough for this breakfast and then I'm broke."

"Don't worry, I'm on the case," he told her as the waitress came around now with their food.

"Here you go sir, and for your friend too," The waitress said.

"Thank you," Andrew interjected as he looked back at Caroline who had received her plate in silence. He spoke up to her again, "Well, do you know where we can take a bus or something back to the other side?"

Indignant again, Caroline roughly expressed to him, "Um, you should know. How else did you get here?"

Andrew was embarrassed again. He did not know how to quite explain his little adventure in getting there, so he carefully crafted an alternate version of his excursion up, "I took the train up last night to Poughkeepsie, stayed at my uncle's in Highland and made my way over here on foot since early this morning."

Caroline did not seem impressed, in fact, she was looking rather stone-faced. She quickly let out a reply, "it sounds like total bullshit, but I'll bite. I have no choice but to follow you I guess."

"Cool," Andrew announced, "So, let's eat."

Andrew was the first to sink he fork into his eggs, but Caroline seemed to take her time. She picked at her food a bit and occasionally looked up to see how Andrew was faring. She prompted him, "Hey, Andrew, tell me, do you have a girlfriend?"

He looked up to her, embarrassingly with a piece of egg hanging from his mouth. He let it drop in surprise and replied to her honestly, "No, no, I, I don't have one. I have too many other things going on."

She smiled at him and asked him suddenly, "So you mean to tell me that such a talented guy such as yourself has no woman. Have you even seen a pair of tits in your life at least, and I don't mean on a magazine."

Andrew bit his tongue by accident and tried not to contort his face, but to no avail. He was shocked and felt this unease and nervous tingle started to radiate over his body. He answered, sucking the blood from his tongue a little, "Ah, no. I've been a bit of good boy if you know what mean. Never had a girlfriend or anything, but Mike and I did see his neighbor's tits once through the telescope, by accident of course."

Caroline laughed. She almost fell out of her chair and looked at Andrew squarely in the eyes and in disbelief told him, "You have never had a woman?"

"No."

"Oh my god. You really are a fucking virgin. I didn't think that there were any left. Well here's what. How about from this day forward you be my boyfriend and I'll be your girlfriend. I will get you up to speed on things, besides, you're cute. How about it, will you go out with me?"

It does not need to be mentioned how wide-eyed Andrew became at this moment, but, could this be real. SHE IS ASKING HIM OUT! There was only one little weak word he could squirm out of his mouth for this occasion, "Okay."

"Cool," Caroline replied, absolutely delighted, "So when we are done here eating lets go somewhere, together, and I know just the place."

"Where," Andrew said, still in dumbstruck.

"To my friend's house up here."

"Alright," Andrew responded and they pressed on with this meal, only now it was he who was picking at his food.

Gray, that was the color of the sky. Andrew and Caroline walked together, holding hands, down the long road towards a town. Walking up the hill as the traffic passed by them, they slowed before a house on what seemed to be the edge of town. It was a rather strange sensation Andrew felt, this was what he had been waiting for, but certainly this was not the way he wanted it to all come together. There was unease in him about how all this was happening. There was something wrong, but most of all, he felt confusion. It was strange and unreal how it was coming together.

"So tell me, how is your family," Caroline asked so casually.

His unease increased, Andrew spoke out to her, "okay, I guess."

She looked up to him and chasten him, "I know more about you than you think. I know you have it rough."

Andrew's eyes picked up and were nervous. He did not speak for a moment, it was so unsettling, her words. His life was something private, and it was highly disturbing that even she would possibly know so much about his life. After the silence, he spoke, "Tell me, what do you know?"

"I know your mother and sister have long been dead and your father is a paraplegic asshole in a wheelchair. I know it's his friends that provide for you, and that you have had a secret crush on me for a whole year. I can tell you a whole lot more stuff, but I think that is all you really need to worry about me knowing."

They stopped and stared into each other's eyes alongside that road. Andrew was at a loss for words. It was like standing naked alongside a busy road, he was ashamed and unclothed; there was no barrel to cover up with. It was profoundly upsetting to him that she would know so much, and still more that she would casually say it to him. His life, his private life, was not something he wanted repeating. It was also not to be treated as ass wiping toilet paper. Here was this woman he had wanted for so long, and now here she is undressing the filthiest parts of him with just her words. He replied to her tersely, "My life is my business. Only my closest friends know so much because they live life with me. How do you know so much about me? Who told you?"

"I am a very good listener, and people can't help but tell me everything," She said so softly, trying to recapture his heart.

"I guess my friends squeal too much," he said to her, making a few educated guesses as to who would say so much about him to her.

"They do, and I am sorry if it bothers you. I was only trying to help." She assured him apologetically.

Andrew looked down for a moment to the ground and stared up again, and looked her in the eye, telling her, "Okay, it's not your fault my friends talk a little too much. Well, I just want you to know this about me, I have a lot of shit going on that I have to always deal with alone, and I would rather have it that way to. People simply do not understand me and everyday is just chock full of more unpleasant things to deal with. That's just the way it is for me. It is no wonder that I would rather be dead most of the time."

"So true," she quickly said as a matter of fact, but then continued, I'm sorry, but that's why I am here. I admire you. I really like you and have liked you. Despite all you have been through you still kick ass with a trumpet, keep scoring the occasional touchdown, and let's admit it, you can be a charmer."

"What do you mean a 'charmer'", he asked her.

"A charmer, I mean, oh come on Andrew, don't you get it," she implored him to understand.

"Get what," he asked rather perplexed.

She seemed to almost pout for a moment but regained her composure and told him, "A charmer. You are a charmer. You can really talk to girls. You talk all nice and everything. You always say all the right words, I mean, you must get A's or something in English."

He never quite looked at himself in that light, but he told her what he could, "I never knew that. I'm good at English, but a, 'charmer?' Where's the proof of that?"

"Hmm. well, you are, so how did you become that way?"

Andrew started walking again, up the gentle hill toward a tree line neighborhood, a pleasant outskirt to a town. Caroline dutifully joined him alongside, "Yea, I guess if you say I speak so well it's just cause I read all the time."

"Really."

"Yea, all those times I had to accompany my dad to the VA hospital, I would bring books and magazines of all kinds cause there is nothing better to do at those places, and of course when I was stuck at home. When you have my father as a parent, you don't go anywhere much of the time, unless you are willing to hoof it everywhere. You just stay where you are. And with no cable and last year's video games, what else can you do other than just read, read, and read. Yes, I am a poor deprived child."

They both smiled at that. Caroline pointed to the entrance of the house ahead of them. They approached and started walking a little faster towards the house. A two-story house it was, tan colored, all vinyl siding. There was a modest front porch that looked unfinished, the naked wood showing all about. Still, it looked quite good and not too shabby. The two of them quickly sneaked up the modest wooden steps and stopped at brown oak door.

"Here we are," Caroline informed Andrew as she cut in front of him and turned the knob of the door to go inside.

"Don't you think we should knock," Andrew asked her as she melted into the inside and he walked in behind her.

The door shut and Caroline began calling out, "Yo, Brianna,

Kayla, girls, where are you." She walked into the room ahead of them calling out their names but no one answered.

With his vision clearing up now after having stepped in so suddenly from the great outdoors, Andrew began studying his surroundings. He was in a red colored room with paisley wallpaper in the background. The rug was a maroon color, and the couches were plaid, like something out of the seventies. In front of the couch was a glass coffee table with an ashtray still containing the remains of a joint and totally finished roach at the end of a small metal clip. A well-used glass bowl, looking much like a glass smoke pipe sat next to it. Numerous shot glasses were strewn about, and by the look of things it was quite apparent that college students live there.

Popping back in from another room, Caroline stepped in. She informed him, "I think they are all gone. It's just us in the house right now." She slowly walked over to him, removing her coat and revealing her voluptuous body, large round breasts, and perfect figure. Andrew was greatly aroused by her as she took her seat on the couch and implored him to do the same on the couch, "Take a seat, relax."

He quickly undid his coat and likewise took a seat. Andrew put his coat aside and looked up to Caroline who was pushing the coffee table aside. Suddenly she knelt down and moved towards him and placed her hand upon his crotch and started to undo his zipper. Andrew suddenly bolted back on his chair and exclaimed to her, "what are you doing. Don't you think it is a little too soon for this."

She looked at him with some puzzlement and asked him, "What, don't you want your dick sucked. Everybody wants their dick sucked, especially by me."

Andrew slid back on the couch as Caroline backed off a little. He announced to her in utter horror, "I am a little uncomfortable with this right now. Can we, like, slow things down just a tad?"

She bolted up and went to sit on a lounge chair opposite the couch. She had a somewhat vacant look on her face and replied to him, "I'm sorry. You really are not like everybody else, but, I'll be honest, and please believe me, all I have ever done is suck dick. I haven't spread my legs or nothing like that. I have my own standards to. Don't get the wrong impression of me."

Andrew was dumbstruck that she could talk so freely about oral sex, but as he sank back down on the couch, he started to feel a bit more at ease, if not a little icky at her, and strangely more aroused than ever at the same time. "Well, it's certainly fast," he exclaimed to her as they both calmed down a bit and looking almost disappointed, Caroline got up and proceeded to sit down next to Andrew. She wrapped her arm around him and cuddle up next to him. Andrew felt a little more pity and likewise held her and they cuddled there for a while. "No, I don't think you are some whore," Andrew let out.

"That's good," Caroline told him, very relaxed. "I just wanted to make things more comfortable. Everybody gives head now-a-days, I wouldn't be surprised if the president's interns give him the same. I don't know why, sometimes, it just makes me feel better so I just do. I haven't sucked that much dick anyway."

Andrew was feeling a little revolted still, but not enough to let go of her, after all, where is he going to find a pure girl in this world. The only thing cleaner than himself is possibly the wind driven snow, and it was not entirely by his choice either but circumstance. Still, his arousal was tempting him so hard now to just let her have her way with him, or vice versa. She is so hot, and luscious. What chance does he ever have to enjoy the pleasure otherwise? Yea, one has to worry about STDs and getting her knocked up, but what the hell, shouldn't he take a chance with her. Why the hell not, he could be dead by noon and never have enjoyed the pleasure. Yes, pleasure was very important now, and it was something that he would hate to let slip through his fingers, but it would change everything, and not necessarily for the better. However it was real. Caroline began to talk to him softly, like a lover now, "you know, sex changes you. It's almost like crack, you get hooked after the first time; you need it in all your relationships afterwards. It kind of sucks, but it's also like having your favorite dish every day whenever you want it. I look at it this way, 'what is so wrong with feeling good?'"

Andrew was listing to her, listing to how casual she was about things. He felt like he spotted a tinge of something wrong in what she said, he found a contradiction. He calmly and intimately let it out, "Is feeling good such a great thing. Is it so good to sit around so doped up that you don't feel a thing while your arms are being cut off? Is it so good to feel so great one day only to wake up the next feeling sick? Why drink and feel sick? Why get high and be imprisoned? Why do things to feel good and pay the consequences later? I think always; it's my bad habit. The one blessing of my lonely life is that I can see, see the things that others can't. I am always looking from the outside in and I see dangers that approach from behind, but when I scream from behind the glass, no one hears me. I see couples fuck, and then I see them break up. I see people drink, and then puke up. I see people get high, and then die. I see life and death, but from a safe enough distance."

"But don't you want to be happy?" Caroline Asked.

"I do, more than anything, but why must all good fun things bring so much pain in the end."

"So go down another road, have fun, live hard, die young and be happy."

"I can't."

"Why not?"

"I don't know, I just feel compelled. There is a storm at the end of the pleasure road and I see it and I don't want to be there when it comes."

"But you are not happy going down your road."

Andrew stopped for a moment and thought. Perhaps she is right. If there is no god, if there is no purpose the storm is going to appear anyway. Everything is the now, no matter how much you try to explain it all away. He might as well have his fun, especially now that he feels Caroline's hand grasping his crotch. How arousing it is now that he is hard like a rock. Time to make a choice, time make his decision. It is quite apparent that this may be his only chance to truly enjoy himself, and have a smile upon his lonely face. This may be his last chance and he is blowing it by worrying about the consequences that he may never live long enough to suffer. There is no god, there is only himself? "The sunset!"

Caroline stopped and now looked to him puzzled at what he just uttered. "The sunset? What the fuck does that have to do with anything?"

Looking straight into space, he told her, "Nothing, nothing much. But looking at them does make me happier. Have you ever stopped and watched one go down? It is like the most beautiful thing. If it clears up today we may be able to watch it go down together."

Mystified, Caroline backed off away from Andrew and sheepishly asked him, "what the fuck are you talking about? The sunset, a sunset, that's it, nothing special with that."

"Yes there is," Andrew implored. "There are things beyond ourselves. There are those things that were here long before us and will be here long after we're gone. I like to look upon those things that have stood the test of time and never fail to disappoint. You know what it is, it is the hope that there is something beyond my few years. There is something eternal about it. I long to look forwards and not backwards, to see what will be, and be inspired by the eternal things. It's the past and present that suck."

"You are strange," Caroline chastised him, belittling him.

Andrew turned suddenly to look at her and was puzzled by her change of mood. Was she not horny just a few moments before? He told her, "We were planning on going home, aren't we?"

"Yea, yea, we were. I thought that we would have a little fun together, though, this is our first day."

Andrew smiled a bit, "I guess so, but isn't that our mission for today."

"Yea."

"Okay, so let's get going." Andrew stood up and grabbed his coat and then asked, "why did we come here anyway?"

"I just thought we would, it was close," Caroline told him.

She just was not acting right. Perhaps she was ill in the head, but there was something contrived about all this. She did not seem all that genuine. "Let's go into town. Maybe we can catch a bus there."

# Chapter 9: the road to nowhere

Drip, drop, drip, drop, that was the sound that the two of them heard everywhere they went. The town was busy with life as many young college folk walked about from store to store like happy little drones. There were various shops with outdoor essentials, like new shinny skis on display, or new multicolored outdoor clothing. Thrift shops seemed to be around every corner with their old clothes presented on the store front windows on time worn mannequins. Tie tied shirts and cardigan sweaters seemed to be the specialties. Every block had a restaurant or two it seemed, with eager eaters inside displaying their many varied sweaters as their coats hung upon chairs, racks and ornate hooks. Still, with every step, there was dripping and the melting of snow as the air temperature climbed well above freezing. They began to descend the hill and into a more densely packed section of town. As they walked down a hill through some more of these little stores they approached a little gas station. Andrew looked at it and saw a brown beat up pickup truck that was parked in front of a pump. Coming out of was a tall, long haired kid with just a flannel shirt and blue jeans on. Caroline seemed to look intently at him and nudged Andrew, "Hey look, it's Brianna's boyfriend, maybe he can take us somewhere instead having to wait around for a bus."

"Okay," Andrew told her as she darted off down the street to talk with the boy. Picking up his pace a little, Andrew stopped and noticed a pay phone at the bus station next to him. Walking over, he started fumbling around for some change. He had this compulsion to call his friend Brian and tell him about what was going on. He had to be home by now, most certainly. Finding his change he started to pile the coins into the payphone and dialed his friend while keeping his eye on Caroline who had now reached the kid and was having quite an animated conversation with him. Andrew looked unconcerned since he knew he was somebody else's boyfriend. Ring, ring, ring, he could hear the phone go through its motions until he heard his friend's voice at the other end.

"Hello."

"Brian, it's me, Stevens, how are you?"

"How are you," Brian told him rather urgently, "Why didn't you tell us your dad was in the hospital. I heard about it from my grandma who stopped by today. She saw him in the hospital ICU. Are you at the hospital right now or something?"

"No, no, I'm not. I'm kinda stuck somewhere right now. Look, I just wanted to know if I made it back later if your parents could give me a lift there from your house?"

"Sure, anything man." At this point Andrew could sense that Caroline was almost done talking to the kid and he hurried it up, "Cool, hopefully I'll see you later, otherwise it will have to wait till tomorrow."

"Okay."

"Catch ya later."

"Alright, peace man." The phone clicked and Andrew hung up. He looked down the street and saw Caroline waving at him to come down and join them at that little gas station by the crappy old pickup. Andrew left the phone and started walking down rapidly towards the two of them, mindful that Brian might be expecting them later, and of course that he had to hurry up getting home. Yet it all deepened on the speed of Caroline and what other detours she might take.

After a short, walk down, Andrew reached the spot where Caroline was talking with this acquaintance. She turned to Andrew with a large smile and happily introduced him to the driver, "Hey, this is Josh, he's my friend Brianna's boyfriend. He' going to take us to my cousin's place to hang there for a little while before we figure out how to get out of this side of the river."

Andrew was a bit puzzled since he assumed that they would just go straight home, but he did not think nothing much of this detour. He replied to the two, "hi, I'm Andrew, Andrew Stevens."

Josh replied in a rather subdued way to him, "Hi, I'm Josh, nice to meet you."

"Well, we're off," Caroline rushed in.

The three of them climbed into the beat up brown pickup and started making their way towards the abode of Caroline's cousin far up into the hills. Andrew got stuck in the middle of the pickup's cab as Caroline sat close to the window and Josh drove.

The rusty old truck backed away from its spot in the gas station puttering back before Josh set gears forward. It lurched away out of the parking lot and onto the main road heading downhill. Ahead against the sunlight could be seen the distant mountains covered in a blanket of white. Quickly the town of New Paltz passed away as the little shops and taverns melted back. They crossed a green cantilever bridge spanning a frozen river. Beyond was an open road surrounded on either side by snow-covered fields that had only but the tallest of the brush poking through the deep layer of snow. To the distance the mountains lay dark and gray against the light of rising Sun. Andrew looked at this and he smiled for he saw that the world was beautiful. The same could not be said for the drive.

The pickup truck was a rather miserable contraption. The cab smelled of dirty socks and every time Josh shifted one could hear the gears grind below. The vehicle felt like it had no shocks for every bump in the road would rattle one's teeth. Andrew bunched himself back into the seat as both Josh and Caroline did not seem to be at all bothered. Josh paid attention to the road and didn't say much while Caroline stared out at the empty space looking out the window at the world pass by emotionless. It was Andrew who was fidgety looking around studying his surroundings, absorbing the new world he was entering. Eventually they departed off the main road and started going up a secondary road that headed towards the mountains. The ride got bumpier as they entered into what seemed to be like a cave of trees devoid of their leaves. The cover was so thick that one could scarcely see the sky through all the barren branches. Just before the road turned steep, a gate of trees on either side imposed its ominous presence. Andrew squeezed himself further back into his seat wondering with dread what he'd gotten himself into on this trip. Caroline for her part in an oddly sadistic way broke the silence and said, "we're getting closer now."

The sudden darkening of the scenery as they were enveloped my tall trees made Andrew more nervous; he was passing a demon army parade in his gut. He felt like he was back in that hiking path with that wretched dog stalking. Just as that memory was about to flood his mind again the trees open up a little and the cab was bathed in the light of the midday sun. There was a clearing up ahead as the road went up another steep hill again. Andrew looked over to his left over Caroline's shoulders and saw in the distance houses hugging the hills covered in a light blanket of snow with some of their chimneys' bellowing gray smoke into the clearing blue skies. The trees stuck up through the snow like hairs on a scraggly old face. The Hill looked however like some citadel from a scary children's story. One could almost presume that a brood of witches and demons would jump from behind the hill but all there was to see were barren trees and the occasional pine coloring the white canvas of winter with some other color than brown and white.

As the crest of the road was reached the road continued through what looked like a tunnel of trees. Peeking through the trees were Driveways completely covered in snow. Most of them on either side looked unplowed, however occasionally there was one that looked plowed. There was one exception however, that was a house to the left. Most of the cabins were new and luxurious, but not this one. It was an odd-looking structure, the rightmost portion of the house was an old two-story farmhouse with the paint peeling off of it. To the left however was a more modern looking addition that was left at only a single story and was rather unfinished. Only bits and pieces of vinyl siding had been mashed on the side but primarily it was the foil back Styrofoam insulation that colored that exterior. In front is a front porch over the older portion of the house that had no guardrails and was composed mostly of grayish rotted looking wood. They pulled into this driveway, an unpaved affair that was noisy from the gravel below it, despite the light covering of fluffy snow.

"We are here," Caroline exclaimed as she opened the door of the vehicle and stepped outside the instant it came to a stop. Caroline slammed the door shut in her wake. Josh quickly followed and left the door open so Andrew could squeeze his way out across the steering column. As soon as Andrew stepped out he was shocked by the sudden cold dryness of the air. It was clean and crisp but brutally freezing. He closed the door behind him and looked around searching for some signs of civilization. He studied his surroundings carefully looked around and took a step forward around the vehicle when he heard a crunching sound from below. He lifted up his boot and looked down to see what was unmistakably broken bits of shattered automotive glass sparkling its distinctive green in the sunlight that penetrated through the thick canopy of trees. He slowly turned to look towards the house to Caroline eagerly knocking at the front door of the house with Josh standing close beside her. Andrew approached cautiously and came to stop before a cinderblock that served as a step to the front porch. He stood sentinel behind Josh and Caroline who had made it up to the door ahead of him. A figure appeared at the door.

"Diane," exclaimed Caroline and she hugged the figure at the door. After she let go she stepped back and you could see who she was. She was a beautiful young blonde, a little bit taller than Caroline and more curvy than her cousin but, nonetheless, magnificently beautiful. Then the young lady proceeded quickly to hugged Josh and greet him with her warm friendly voice. Caroline then pointed to Andrew and introduced him to her, "this is my new boyfriend Andrew."

Diane stepped forward and down the steps to greet Andrew shook his hand, "hi, it's really nice to meet you, I didn't know Carolina found herself a boyfriend."

"Well I guess she's full of surprises," Andrew said a bit uncomfortable but pleased to see this beautiful young lady.

"Well come on in then, we got lots to do."

Stepping inside the house one could smell the strong scent of burning cedar, an odd but wonderful smell that is soothing like a hot cup of coco on a cold winter's day like this. The house was not very rich at all but in fact quite humble. The paneling on the walls was quite cheap and reminiscent of something out of the 70s. The furniture was old and worn, to the left of what looked like an impromptu living room, and it was the newest looking of the rooms were the paneling was quality wood slats. The couch was worn threadbare and was stained from years of use. A well-worn coffee-table, rather disgusting though, sat in the middle with many old dirty shot glasses piled on it with an overflowing ashtray whose tobacco smell was only apparent when you approached it. To the right was a staircase that went upstairs and next to it a doorway into an area that was covered over with plastic that had begun to discolor from age and smoke. To the side was a dining room, the walls painted an off white shade and an old looking dinner table surrounded by folding chairs. A simple gun rack was bolted to the wall, devoid of its rifle or shotgun, covered in dust from lack of use. By the slight smell of something cooking, like chicken soup, one could detect that the kitchen was nearby, perhaps just behind the wall of living room or more towards the back by the dining room area.

As Diane and Caroline melted away into another room Andrew stood where he was alone in the living room before the threadbare couch. He plopped himself down on the couch and began to look around the room and investigate its various attributes. He looked to his left and saw an old TV set that had a video game console on top with a control pad dangling from the side. Below it was a TV stand filled with more games and movies, some of which he could see were clearly pornographic. To his right is the entrance way where he came into the house and looked at the staircase and the various pictures on it as it let its way upstairs. Beyond that sealed off room with plastic he could only wonder what was under construction. He looked around and he saw that there were various pictures on the wall, most of them of Diane and her family. There was nothing particularly special about them, if anything they looked contrived, things taken by a photographer in the studio but nothing more. Finally, his eyes fell upon the coffee table in front of them and the filthy shot glasses on it. Some of them had the dried-out sugar from schnapps sticking to the walls of the glasses. Andrew looked more carefully in the piles of glasses and plastic cups and saw something that truly disturbed him and bothered him. It was something that was enough to arouse his suspicion about the situation. There, by lonely little glass is a little trace of fine white powder with a cut out straw and razor next to it. He knew what it was, cocaine and it was bad enough that Caroline enjoyed a little marijuana, but a hard drug like that cocaine was something not to be trifled with in his world. Suddenly Caroline appeared again at the front of the room and asked Andrew what he was looking at, "what are you staring at."

Andrew looked up to her with a rather blank expression and asked, "do you guys snort coke?"

Carolina instantly developed an annoyed frown on her face and said to him, "Do I look like a coke head? Am I always sniffling, no! So what if there is coke here, life should be fun. You should do what you want, do as you will, and let nothing stand in your way. At the end of the day life is short so you might as well enjoy it. You gotta stop being such a pussy."

He was a little disturbed by her words and retracted a bit into the seat and told her, "when I was a little kid and I ran out into the street after a ball, there was my grandmother to grab me by my collar before I got run over by a car. If I had done as I will I would've been dead. You can't always do what you want. You got a look around, look at the whole picture if you don't want to die some miserably pathetic death. Of course, if you don't care..."

Caroline interrupted violently and told him, "no, survival of the fittest, smart people always come through and survive every time. That is just the way life is."

Now Andrew became annoyed, and he grew angry because he loved his grandmother and he argued back," that's fine and dandy for you but I loved my grandmother and she loved me. She kept me alive because she wanted me to live long enough to be happy. You can't do that if you're dead!"

Carolina instantly changed her expression and became a little bit more charming in reply to Andrew, "well I'm sorry that you feel that way. I didn't mean to insult your grandmother but philosophically I have my own way of living."

Andrew asked quite inquisitively, "what would you do if someone proved you wrong about your way of living?"

"There is no such thing, it's all relative."

Andrew, ever the nerd replied back, "and yet the speed of light is constant despite what frame of reference you look at it from."

Suddenly Caroline developed a confused look on her face and could only muster to him a simple response, "What are you talking about? The hell does that have to do with anything?"

Feeling suddenly triumphant Andrew barked at her, "facts Caroline, facts."

Caroline started biting her lip and slowly made her way over next to Andrew and sat down beside him and leaned her head on his shoulder. She told him in a rather innocent way, "you know, you are so smart, I'm glad I picked you to be a boyfriend."

Andrew gently asked her, "Did you learn anything?"

She looked up to him and gave him a wicked smile and said, "I don't need to really learn anything, but maybe later I'll be able to show you things." She gave him a wink and Andrew winked back at her, but he understood in his mind she implied something profoundly sexual, and she did arouse him greatly, again, however that nasty little instinct for survival prodded him think beyond that. In the pit of his stomach an ache of suspicion was building ever more. Diane returned into the room with a rather deep tray in one hand and a moist rag on the other. She immediately walked over to the coffee table, bent low, and started rapidly pushing everything into the tray in an effort to quickly clean up the coffee table while a decorative bowie knife fell on the floor. She looked up and momentarily acknowledge them.

"Don't worry guys, I'll clean this up soon and get us some drinks." Andrew was still busy looking at Caroline, studying the perfect features of the perfect face, looking into those deep blue eyes and forgetting for a moment that discomfort building inside. Yet there was something wrong with them, there was something wrong with those eyes of her. He found something frighteningly lifeless and vacant about her. He looked at her and all he saw was an almost statuesque form, she looked almost lifeless, and there was a lifelessness that penetrated through her physical beauty that only became apparent with increased familiarity. As Diane continue to clean up the living room with that wet rag of hers, Andrew's mind spilled into his words as he expressed this sentiment as gently as he put it.

"Have you ever looked at a dead animal. Have you ever intently stared at its corpse? Have you ever walked into an art gallery and felt spooked by all the lifeless statues and portraits around you? I once went to a department store with my grandmother to shop in a store was closing down, I think it was the old Alexander's in White Plains. I wandered away from her for a while and I found myself amongst all these mannequins; here they were these painted lifelike forms of nude women with what could've been voluptuous and beautiful bodies yet I was spooked by these forms, I saw them for lifeless statues that they were and it was scary. They were unnatural and I could feel that. I ran away from that spot through the empty store and found my grandmother and hugged her in tears. That was the first time I acknowledged the creepiness of, 'the uncanny valley.' Just as you can feel the holiness emanate from a genuinely good person in the room, when an evil thing comes in to my presence I feel and see a certain emptiness that sucks out all life out of me; I fell a very unnatural, how should I put it, death. I've been to funerals before and no matter how well you fix up the body, you cannot hide how dead it is."

"You know what I say Andrew," Caroline assured him softly, "fuck it."

"I'll be back with some drinks, "Diane suddenly said as she swiftly exited the living room.

Andrew was looking down at Caroline more critically. Caroline suddenly stopped leaning on his shoulders and righted herself up on the couch. She looked up and out into space and did not utter a word. Andrew was baffled by this and felt increasingly repulsed at a Caroline. Caroline suddenly turned to him and flashed him another seductive look and asked him, "what do you do to take your mind off life?"

Andrew developed a rather inquisitive look on his face and thought hard for a moment and told her quite honestly, "I live. Play my horn, hang with my friends, do a lot of reading, but I can never take my mind off life. I can only live it, or at least, I choose to, so far."

Caroline stared at him with disgust and instructed him, "you need to get laid and then we need to see to it that you get properly medicated too."

Andrew felt like rolling around his eyes, she did not get it. Before he could comment any further Diane returned into the room. She returned with multiple shot glasses full of their amber liquor. She brought them in with such balance all nestled on her arm against her alluring breasts that one must image she was a skilled waitress. Underage though he was, Andrew was no stranger to Alcohol and relished a good strong drink once in a while when the opportunity presented itself, but always in moderation. Andrew reached out for the fluid form the shot glass she held in her hand as she flashed a smile to him with her kind, roundish face. She was so comforting and unthreatening to Andrew's eyes. Caroline followed behind with a straight, almost annoyed look to her face. She was beautiful as ever, but had that look upon her that lacked any joy and stood in contrast to her actions. Diane was very cheerful and happy, she was a contrast from Caroline who seemed more sever, cold and calculating at times; or at least that was the impression that Andrew got. She reached out to Diane to grab a drink as she put her hand on Andrew's leg and likewise he did the same almost as reflex. They looked at each other and each smiled, but awkwardly. He was uncomfortable all of a sudden and felt like he was almost doing something bad. There was something in his mind that was trying to pick out the logic of what might be wrong with all this, but he endured, if for no other reason than he was in the presence of two beautiful women and was trying to be a polite guest. There was that nagging feeling in him, still, that this was all too fast, that this was wrong. He should not be holding onto her leg at all, but then again they were so smooth. Diane finally took a seat and began to converse, "So, how did you to meet, tell me the details." Diane was so curious; childlike in a way.

Caroline let out large flush smile at Andrew, making sure her eyes met his, Andrew was not so enchanted as before, he was starting to develop a bad taste. She turned to Diane and told her, giddy like a schoolgirl, "I've known Andrew for a while, through friends of course. He goes to Stepinac; he's pretty popular there." Andrew cringed a little at that notion because he knew the truth better. Caroline continued, "Andrew is really cool, he plays football, varsity, and made all county or something like that. He also plays the trumpet. He plays so awesome, it's ridiculous. Isn't that right Andrew." She nudged him a bit with her elbow, and it embarrassed Andrew a little. Yes he was a Football player and a damned good one at that, and yes he was the finest Trumpet player the school had ever seen, but he knew she could never really have known that first hand because he never saw her go to one of his concerts, and one had better believe that he would known it if he saw her at one. Caroline continued with her diatribe and persisted to lie, "Oh and Andrew drives the girls wild back home. I am lucky to have gotten him. He comes from a good family, his dad is a war hero or something, right?"

Andrew had sunk back into the couch, embarrassed. Not that he did not mind that Caroline propped him up before an attractive stranger, but what would be Diane's impression when she discovered it to be nothing more than a series of embellishments. People would think that he had lied to Caroline rather than her massaging the truth on her own. Granted some of it was true and some of it false, but nonetheless it all seemed just plain false in the end. He did speak for himself finally when she spoke of his dad, "Yes, my dad was a war hero once, they gave him the air force cross. Four and half air to air kills in Vietnam. But what good is that when he is nothing more than a shadow of his former self. My father was a great soldier once and now he is nothing. Since that accident that killed my mother and sister, two people I've never had the pleasure of knowing all I've grown up with is a paraplegic, insufferable, miserable little man who sometimes doesn't know the difference between the 60s and the 90s. Sometimes he doesn't know that I'm his own son, maybe just one of the home health aides that drop by ever so once in a while to take care of him. I don't have it very easy, and certainly I wish I knew the brave fighter pilot, the successful lobbyist and great somebody that he once was but my reality with him sucks. I have been miserable all my life at home. My grandparents took care of me when I was a child and loved me but I had to bury them. I have my father's friends taking care of me, teaching me things and letting me travel around the world, but at the end of the day I come back to my miserable little home. I can't escape Port Chester, I can't escape Smith Street, I can't escape my rotting old house that smells more like a nursing home than a family dinner. I think I can speak for myself!" Andrew forcefully said at the end as he stared daggers into Caroline's eye and down at his hands, seeing that they had moved away from her leg and turned into a clenched fist.

Both Caroline and Diane retracted a bit into their respective places and kept their quiet. Diane developed a nervous look on her face while Caroline's face turned into an almost evil frown for a moment. Immediately, though, she reclined again in her position and returned a blank expression to her face. Andrew looked at her intently and noticed her facial contortions. He saw a diabolical something in here at that moment. His fists let go for a moment and focused his eyes into hers and bored into her with them like lasers and asked her with a quiet ferocity, "You don't care that I was made upset. You don't care about anything, do you."

Charming as ever, she replied to him, "no, no, I did not mean to not care. Sorry about my look too, I was just a little shocked by your temper. I've never seen that side of you and it made me nervous."

She returned that blank expression to her face after looking so concerned for a moment. Andrew sat back and smirked. After a moment of silence, Andrew, well reclined in his spot addressed them, "So, what do we do for the day. Eventually we need to go, 'home?'"

Diane who had sat quietly and nervous got up and voiced to the two, "We can play cards and have some drinks. I'll go get the deck and some chips." She walked off quickly and nervously while Andrew and Caroline seemed to stare daggers at each other. Caroline got up herself, slowly and seductively, shaking her hip a little to the side and blowing Andrew a kiss turning to follow her cousin. Andrew did not wink or even so much as move. His eyes just followed her off the room, un-amused. Something happened at this point, something important. He had lost his "love," for her and suspicion reigned.

# Chapter 10: Reverse Walpurgisnacht

The bong was being passed around the room, a simple contraption they had made from a soda bottle and a random piece of PVC pipe and foil. Caroline and Diane passed amongst themselves, wearing out a lighter along the way. Andrew declined. He always declined such pleasures, he very much liked having his mind be perpetually sharp, hence why he detested being even drunk, his internal agitation did not appreciate being slowed down.

Instead of the remnants of cocaine lines like earlier there were playing cards on the table along with a burning scented votive candle; lavender it was. Blackjack was the game since the girls really did not know of any other card game. Andrew on the other hand was a card shark and spent the night collecting from the girls all their pennies and other assorted change. While the girls toked away, Andrew sat blissfully content on making the girls a little bit poorer. There also was plenty of alcohol to be had but he only consumed two shots of whiskey. He had gotten himself drunk before with his friends and he did not wish to make himself feel sick especially since there was something inside of him that did not trust the girls at all tonight. Caroline and her cousin laughed and laughed the night away and seem to be blissfully happy even as Andrew pretty much won all of their money. This was the state of affairs when Andrew suddenly broke into a conversation. "So, tell me, girls, what shall we do now that I've exhausted all of your change." Andrew quickly looked at the clock hanging over the mantel place and saw that it was nearing seven o'clock that evening, and it had been dark out now for hours.

Diane, responded to Andrew, "I don't know but maybe my girl here does." Diane and Caroline started to whisper into each other's ears and then bolted towards the upstairs. Diane looked at Andrew quickly as she was leaving and told him, "stay right where you are."

"I'm not going anywhere," Andrew responded to Diane and gave him a quick smile and left with Caroline into another room.

Andrew was different. His mind was not concerned with

sex, or possession of anything. He was concerned now with simply getting back to his home. He wanted to sleep in his own bed. No matter how much Caroline and Diane distracted Andrew, he kept coming back to one thought prevailing in his mind now, getting home. He had money in his wallet but he really had no means of leaving. For that matter he scarcely had a clue of where he was at all. It was wintertime and it was already dark outside and these roads are a mystery to him. He heard the girls giggling in another room opening and closing drawers when the noises suddenly died down. Even though he did not drink much, he still had a taste for whiskey and reached over to the table next to the cards were a big bottle Jack was sitting, almost empty. There was probably still enough for a couple of more shots and so he poured himself a shot on one of the several whiskey glasses strewn all about the room. He lifted a shot glass to his mouth took a whiff before he let his lips touch that amber liquid. Andrew drank it down slowly and he thought to himself for a moment what it would be like to live an adult life on his own and not be burdened like he is now. It would at least be nice if he could put the old unused Cadillac on the road. Wouldn't it be nice, also, to be able to openly drink a shot of whiskey without worrying about the legality of it? Yet as he finished it he said to himself, "is this the meaning of life? Do we live solely to entertain ourselves, or is there more to live for, a lot more?" At that thought he heard a commotion as the girls descended.

Diane was dressed in the bathrobe and nothing underneath while Caroline was stark naked. Her body was absolutely incredible, her breasts plump and succulent; sweetest of fruits. She has the most lurid and seductive look imaginable on her face, but so horribly out of place. She walked right up to Andrew and pushed him against the couch looking into his eyes with her fiery eyes she declared to him, "I am going to fuck the living shit out of you. You need a serious deflowering."

Andrew recoiled in his seat and both turned on and disturbed at the same time. Diane had also gotten up and stripped herself of the bathrobe to reveal her equally voluptuous body. Andrew, however, was not ready for sex. He was not ready for any of this, he was only wanted to go home. He sheepishly asked Caroline, "You want a threesome!"

"It's time we break you in, boy." Caroline told him as she thrust her hand into his crotch and began massaging his testicles.

Andrew wiggled his way aside and implored to her, "I can't do this. I can't do this. This is not me. I am not meat!" Andrew managed to push Caroline aside and he stood up boldly before them. He declared to them, "I want to go home. That's why I came all the way over here, to find a way home."

Caroline peered down angrily at Andrew and with a frown on her face scolded him, "are you a faggot, a herb! What the fuck, you will fuck me, you will fuck me and her and be a man. I want to Fuck and I will FUCK!"

Diane was taken aback by her cousin's angry reaction. Diane stepped forward and actually maneuvered to stand in front of Andrew and began to implore with her cousin, "I think maybe we should leave him alone. He seems to be an alright kind of kid."

Caroline looked a bit infuriated but she suddenly changed her demeanor and grabbed the robe that Diane had tossed aside and put it on slowly. She bound herself tightly with it and declared, "yeah, I think we'll leave him alone.... for now." Caroline stormed upstairs as Diane went looking for something to put on. She started to apologize to Andrew, shaking her head at what had transpired as she threw on a random shirt that was lying about, "I'm sorry, but you know, she gets that way sometimes. I mean, I have never met a guy that did not want to fuck before. I thought you were playing with us, playing hard to get or something. I mean, that's what she kept on telling me upstairs."

Andrew continued to stand where he was and explained himself from the depths of his soul, angry and cold but still under control, "I do not play around like that. I care about myself and those around me. I may joke to my friends that I would do this chick or the other, but truth is that I will know who I want to be with, when I want to do it, and have it be something meaningful, not like a God damned Dog in the street. Sex is not a game, not to me. I see young girls get knocked up, I've got one kid on my block with AIDS, and the tears from my friends after the deed and the confusion. You can't take back that innocence, you can't be carefree anymore, and your relationships will never be the same. We are not adults. We don't have the wisdom, knowledge or money to deal with the consequences. I just don't want to do something I will regret the rest of my life simply cause my dick wants to. I am not my penis, I am me! I think before I act because I choose to live."

Diane, almost penitently replied to him, "I am sorry. I just do things cause they feel right, and Caroline's the same way. We just do it."

"But don't you think about what you are doing," Andrew admonished her.

"No."

"Why?"

Looking up she told him in such an innocent way, "Because it is too hard. It's too hard to have to think about everything you do. It makes you feel dirty and guilty sometimes. I guess that is why so many girls cry after their first time. It's just because they think about it. I always just did what I wanted and tried not to think about it later. I try not to care about it. It makes all the pain go away."

Still strong and with authority Andrew said, "I choose to think about it because I want a different tomorrow. I am not a slave and I will not be a slave to myself. If you like life and want to live it helps to think about what you do, doesn't it? Pain is the best teacher, don't try to run away from it."

"But you see, we don't care. Life is short, let's enjoy it."
She gave him a little smile.

He gave her a remark. "But you don't have to send death an
invitation, and you don't have to take everybody with you on your
twisted road to hell."

A voice suddenly penetrated through the room, that of
Caroline. She silently made her way back downstairs dressed as if
she was ready to go out, dressed in clean pair of jeans and a cardigan
sweater. She had in her hand a small mirror covered in powder that
undoubtedly was cocaine. She tossed it aside and walked into the
room and told them, "I teach you, Andrew Thomas Stevens, the
truth. The truth is that you don't need to worry about anyone other
than yourself. Who cares if you live or die? I don't need you
messing around with my cousin's head. Everything and everyone
here is my bitch! So tell me something,' boyfriend,' do you have any
money?"

Andrew frowned and asked her, "Why?"

"Because that is all you're useful for. You know as the two
of you talked and I got myself dressed and got myself high and I
realized that you were good for something. I realized you came up
here alone and nobody really knows you're up here and I know you
have money since you paid for everything. So I figured since you
are listening to our conversation earlier today that now would be a
good time to make you useful."

Andrew was disgusted and he told her, "Hey, I'm not meat,
bitch, so go back upstairs and sleep it off you fucking cokehead, and
liar!"

Caroline stepped forward, closer into the room and that's
when Andrew noticed she had something in her other hand. It was a
machete and looked primed to kill. She snapped up quickly pointed
only a few feet away from Andrew right up towards his face and
told him, "I know you heard us talk about what we did this weekend,

I will not let you get away and talk about it."

Diane tried to jump in and stop her cousin and implored her, "please don't say it, don't say it."

"Shut up," Caroline screamed, "shut the fuck up, he knows, he knows I killed my father this weekend. I know he saw the car in the woods, that black little car. And now that we are all here alone we will kill him. We will use his money. We will do whatever we want when we want and I will not let him stop me from doing my will!"

"No," Diane yelled as she grabbed the lamp by the couch to bat away the blade which flew off into another room. Suddenly Caroline lunged at her cousin they both fell to the ground and slugging it out on the ground, knocking over the table and the votive candles fell form their perch and shattered on the ground, igniting the couch. They both started reaching over for the knife that had fallen on the ground before. Andrew seized his chance and grabbed his coat and hat to run outside. He looked quickly over at the two fighting on the ground and dashed out the front door. He started running outside into the dark night away from the madness inside that house. He turned back and looked at the house and saw Caroline, her clothes stained in blood. She stood there with the bloody blade. Andrew's breath billowed into the cold dark night, obscuring this nemesis for a moment. But from the smoke again she emerged and stepped out into the cold with the blade in her hand. Her breath was like that of a dragon and her eyes pierced like swords in the night. The ghostly crescent moon up above illuminated the night and snowpack. Caroline gave demonic grin, a grin no human could give willingly. Andrew ran down into the dark road, picking up speed with his feet, and he heard from behind the wicked cry of Caroline as she yelled out to him in her demonic way, "Come back here little boy, I only want to kill you, and maybe piss on your body when I am done!" He ran further and tripped and fell upon a rut on the road. Looking back towards the house he saw Caroline's black outline against the eerie glow of the exterior house light now blazing like a search light from hell. She had descended from her throne of flame and began heading towards him like a film slasher. That black menacing outline was armed with the large blade that fallen to the floor earlier. Caroline suddenly started running in his direction and Andrew picked himself up and ran down the road again. The scene has become brilliantly illuminated in the orange glow of the burning house. The cold air made his breath billow like a runaway locomotive. He descended down the hill and ran at full fury, again tripping. Caroline, he felt, was catching up, but he could not look. He had to keep on moving forwards and the further he went, the blacker it became, and he hoped, hoped for some real light.

A few more yards now and he saw a light; he saw two beams of a pickup rolling up the road and the sound of an old engine. As he looked down he started waving frantically for the car stop. He ran up, only seeming those two round lights come up and stop before him. He ran around the brown pickup began banging incessantly on the window, yelling for help, "Help, help, you got to help me!"

Andrew quickly stepped back as the door opened and saw none other than the young man who driven him up there in the first place get out of the car. Josh laid his hands on Andrew's shoulders and shook him, imploring of him, "Dude, what is going on, what's happened to the girls?"

"It's Caroline, it's Caroline, she's gone crazy." Andrew frantically tried to let out. Suddenly the sound of running feet approached them and Josh looked over to see it was Caroline.

He yelled at her, "Caroline, stop, stop." It was too late for Caroline quickly drove the knife into him, and pulled it out of him as he fell. Andrew bolted immediately down the hill like a frightened animal.

She yelled out at Andrew, "Come back here to the house. Let me gut you like a fish. I am not going to let anyone put me away. I will live my life how I want to live it boy, even to death!

You hear me! To death!"

Andrew continued his run down the hill but the light grew dimmer and dimmer till soon the burning house was nothing more than the dim dot in the eerie, still calm night. Not too long after he hear the sounds, wretched sounds of the pickup being revved, and as he looked back he saw two lights clumsily swing around from their pivot point and start heading down the road. He stopped for a moment and knew he had to break one way or the other to avoid being struck by the vehicle. As he saw the lights approaching, he had to do something drastic, something to survive and make a choice, perhaps a deadly one. He looked away from the approaching truck and saw beyond the woods in the distance on what looked like a hill several small lights, perhaps from some houses. He swallowed hard and dashed into the dark brush towards them not knowing through the black forest if he could reach them in time before he would freeze to death in the dark.

# Chapter 11: Sacrifice of the unknown soldier

Light, light from the moon glow descended upon the earth, calmly, and still. The reflection off the snow on the ground illuminated the dark night and helped Andrew move along. He moved as quickly as he could through the barren brush and snow, trying to find an alternate path and some sign of civilization. As the hour progressed, Andrew became more and more tiered, and his legs stiffer and stiffer. His feet were tired, wet, and cold though the adrenaline kept them from freezing over. Soon he moved through the brush with plodding steps on the ground. Eventually he stopped and leaned against a tree and took a good look around. He was going up yet another hill. He was getting dangerously sweaty. Soon hypothermia would set in and he would die. Time now was the enemy, every bit as much as the bitterly cold night and Caroline. His only hope was that a house would be around the corner, or that this night had already consumed Caroline. Whatever the case may be he continued with his last bit of strength, but the cold was not just biting, it was feasting on him.

There was a smell in the air, burning wood. He knew what this could mean. There was some house nearby, a phone, some help. He walked a little further and the smell became overpowering, there was a house nearby and warmth with it. He moved up the hill a little more and stumbled over a few branches and found himself on a lonely dirt road. It was frozen and hard as a rock, painful to fall upon, but it was an encouraging sign. He picked himself up and looked both ways to spot a place he could go. He looked now towards the clear skies to hopefully find a plume of smoke breaking over the stars like a translucent gray blanket. Looking over to his right he found the source a hundred yards away and trudged his tired body towards it with a renewed vigor. Every step fell hard upon the ground and he could feel his body shivering now as the cold penetrated his clothing, but he continued and tried desperately to fight off the urge to fall asleep where he stood. Yet, he triumphed and he saw the outline of a property, and soon a looming shadow of a cabin. Next to it, before he got to it, he could see a driveway, but to his utter disappointment there were no cars in it. The house stood alone and darkened. The wood stove however was going, no doubt keeping it warm. As he walked now onto the property, he could see jetting out from the back of the house the source of the smoke, a small shed with a stainless-steel chimney on top that looked like a pointed hat. The now wonderful aroma of burning wood came from it, and warmth emanated from around the structure. From it a large stainless-steel tube wrapped in insulation about a foot wide ran to the house just a few feet away. It was not a perfect source of heat, but it was sufficient to keep him alive. He could see around the bottoms that the snow had melted away hinting that it was leaking heat. It was probably a good forty degrees hotter next to that air duct than away from it. Andrew however knew that he had to hide in order to keep himself alive. He looked around for something to cover himself with and found next to shed a blue tarp that covered a cord of wood. It was held down by a trio of bricks so Andrew quietly moved them aside and pulled the tarp away from the cord of wood. He took that tarp and covered himself with it as he lay down on the ground against the furnace by a particularly warm spot where the ducting exited, wrapping himself up in it so as to make it look like he was more akin to a covered piled of wood than a young man. He pulled his shoes off and socks and placed them in a particularly warm spot in hopes now that they would dry. Now warmer and totally exhausted he quickly fell asleep.

A crash and shattering glass was heard. Andrew awoke startled and had a cold shiver run down his spine. He lay where he was motionless, still covered completely by the tarp. A concern blew over him, but he collected his senses and waited patiently for the noises to stop. A few more seconds later and he heard a car fire up and the sound of grinding gears, like that of an old truck. Hearing nothing approaching him, he quickly slid out from under the tarp, ready to run, when curiosity got the better of him and so he silently slipped on his now dry socks and shoes; he stood up and moved quickly to the corner of the house to see to whom the vehicle belonged. With his eyes slowing sliding along the side of the timber wall of the house, he finally peered into the driveway and saw the truck, the beat-up brown truck with Caroline as a driver. Next to her was a shot gun and red shotgun shells strewn over the dashboard. She clumsily continued to back up the car, clearly unfamiliar with driving stick. Soon enough she made a quick J turn back and stopped the vehicle for a while, moments spent figuring out how to put the car in gear. Suddenly, the truck staggered forwards and she was off down the road again from where Andrew had come the night before. Andrew waited a good five minutes standing in that spot, waiting to see if she would return, but she did not and, so, he made his move forwards. He carefully walked around the perimeter of the house and towards the front door. Caroline must have muscled her way in with something and saw on the floor a pole pounder that she must have secured from somewhere. The frame was broken into splinters around where the door lock was; presumably that was where she pounded the door in. Andrew walked inside carefully, but with a careful step. It ran through his mind that he did not want to be accused of having broken into someone's house.

He looked around and saw the house was orderly and almost untouched. There was a coat of dust everywhere inside the house, save for the area between the front door and what looked like a thermostat. The house was divided inside. Ahead was a small hallway that apparently led to a kitchen in the darkened back of the house. To the right was a living room and the left a doorway towards a dining room. To the immediate left was a staircase that went upstairs. Andrew walked into the living room and saw that there was a large fish tank embedded into the wall that was illuminated. Unfortunately, the tank had been smashed and water was all over the floor with exotic fish now still and dead on the oak floor with the lone exception of a clown fish still twitching a little, helpless on the ground. Ahead of him was a faux fireplace that had a nice mantel built around it, but quickly his eyes maneuvered to the walls where he saw pictures. He saw black and white pictures of a young soldier, army it looked like, smiling back at him. He looked around and saw other mementos of war, as well as a variety of little medals and memorabilia. He could tell the owner must be in the American Legion or something. His curiosity again went back to the mantel place where he looked above and saw a gun rack. On the lowest rung there was a rifle or shotgun missing. A box of shells below had been opened and emptied of its contents. It sat alone on top of the mantle, its side open. However, above that empty rack was another weapon, a Rifle, and not any rifle, but from its time worn wooden stock, and blued steel receiver and barrel, what could only be a vintage world war two M1 rifle. It still had its old green sash and a full clip of 30.06 rounds in a pouch affixed to the wood stock. Andrew walked up to the rifle and tried to reach for it but it was mounted too high for him. For that matter he would have had a hard time reaching for the shotgun, if it was still there. It was Obvious why Caroline had gotten the shotgun; it was the only one she could reach. Andrew reached up and tried again to reach for that rifle but he would not reach it; he strained on his toes to get to it. Disappointed he looked around the room for something to stand on and looked over at the couch that was against the front wall of the house. Before that was a coffee table made of sturdy hard wood. Andrew walked over to it and pulled it over before the mantel, it made a horrible screeching noise as he dragged it across. Satisfied with its position, Andrew stepped onto it and now reached over the mantel. The table he could feel begin to tip over but soon his fingers grabbed hold of the receiver and he pulled the gun down, jumping off the table before it tipped over. He now had a weapon, he now had hope.

A creak, he turned and looked, suddenly Andrew was seized with terrible anxiousness. Andrew stood still and heard another creak, but it was on the floor below him, it was nothing more than the house settling. He breathed a sigh of relief and noticed another room around the corner. He walked up and peered into it. It was a study with a lonely desk in it along with other war mementos dotting the walls. Next to desk was a large mirror on the wall, narrow but tall. It was decorated with some pen marks on the side, given the little dates that were written on it with permanent marker, Andrew presumed them to be measurements of children and grandchildren growing up. Andrew chuckled to himself a little, but in good fun. It was a positive sign of life, a positive sign of normality. It flooded his mind with memories of his grandparents, mostly on his mother's side, who did such little things. Those times have since long past. Soon, though, he looked at his reflection in the mirror. He turned a little and looked at himself with that rifle. There was something funny about all this. Here he was in dress pants, a trench coat, old hat, black leather gloves and an M1 Garand slung over his shoulder. He paused for a moment before the mirror and saw something in himself, an image that worked from the deepest part of his soul to his very eyes for a moment, a moment that would remain suspended in time. He saw himself as a soldier, his coat turning an olive drab and woolen, his shoes into black combat boots and a well-worn olive drab helmet on his head. He looked into his eyes, and he saw a soldier, a solider just trying to survive. And just as suddenly as that imaged appeared, it vanished from his head; he was left now just starring at his tired young self.

Shaking his head at what he believed to be a day dream, he realized that he had to get out of there. He looked around some more and spotted a note on ground. He stooped down to pick it up, the rifle slung tightly over his shoulder; he read it and saw it was an invoice for services, apparently from some property management company, which could explain why an empty house was being heated. Perhaps the owner just hired them to heat the house and keep his expensive fish alive, but it looks as if Caroline did a good job of ruining that. He chuckled to himself again, but this time at the comedy and tragedy of Caroline. So evil was she that all life meant nothing to her. For that matter she would extinguish it wherever she went, and probably for no other reason than her own sick entertainment. It was petty, it was ugly, but it was the truth of what she was. Now under stress and desperate, all her pent-up evil shown. Of course, Andrew knew he had a task to do, a mission of sorts to accomplish now. He walked out again into the living room and looked up at that picture of that once young soldier. He looked at that picture of the young man, probably no older than himself when he went out to war to fight against the greatest evil the world had ever known. Now here he was going off to a different war, to fight against a different devil with that same old rifle. He spotted a dark blue knit cap, a beret of sorts sitting lonely on the couch. It was simple and time worn, long enough for him to stretch over his almost cold ears. He grabbed it and put it on, a measure to keep himself warm. There was also a pair of green woolen gloves that sat nearby on a stand that were faded and thin, but still serviceable. He slipped them on since his were still wet with sweat. He looked up again at that picture, at that picture of the young man who went to war so many years ago so he could be free and said to it, "I won't let you down sir. I won't let you down." He saluted it like a good soldier and quickly made his way out of the house.

The snow started falling, heavy now. Andrew began walking quickly, up the road and back where he came from. He was not running away from Caroline, no, he was resolved now to hunt her down and bring her to justice. He was going to expose her to the light of day and he was not going to stop till he had won this personal victory. He walked with a determined look on his face, though he felt sore and tired he pictured in his mind, and heard in his ears the battles and sacrifices of the Unknown Soldier whose rifle he carried. He was going out to war now in an effort to change this little corner of earth. He was going to do it not just to save himself from that evil seductress, but everyone else who may end up in her path. He had decided he was going to do something more with his life than running away. It was all he could do to honor the someone like Unknown Soldier.

# Chapter 12: The braver choice

Two tracks were left on the ground from where Caroline had driven. A thin fluff of snow had now started collecting on them, soon ready to obscure them. This was not the time for Andrew to hesitate, he knew he had to make his move now. He could not run from her. He was going after her.

"Fuck her," he said to himself, and assured himself of success defeating her. "I'll win," he repeatedly to himself consistently, every few minutes reassuring himself of his newfound destiny, as the slayer of the beast. He moved and started walking up the hill fast and most deliberately. He developed a cadence to his step and practically marched on to battle. Cold fluffy white snowflakes collected upon him, his hat and coat being covered by them as the cold wind blew and reduced visibility. The hill got steeper and harder to climb but he continued on, fueled with the will to survive and defeat her. Somewhere out there was the succubus, driving around aimlessly searching for her prey, only now the prey turned hunter. An hour, two hours and three hours passed as time seemed to vanish. It was hard to see anything around him but he was not deterred. By the fourth hour the snow stopped and the wind began to blow hard again, this time from the west. Clarity returned to the environment and the skies began to clear. The temperature however dropped and his breath billowed like an angry locomotive. He pushed back the safety on the rifle, listening for its click and pulled on the op rod to load the chamber. He lifted the sight up near the receiver and readied for action. He was very familiar with rifles; his father's friend long ago taught him how to shoot one back when he was a freshman in High School. He went hunting on safari with that gentleman; he practiced shooting on a 30-03 Enfield. He was to say the least an outstanding shot. He beat his father's friend, an old Marine sniper in a friendly dual over the savanna, and took down a raging lion with a perfect head shot between the eyes. With this memory in mind, he walked over with the weapon in hand, positioning it in firing position, checking over his shoulder every few moments to make sure no one would get the drop on him. "Got to get to higher ground," he said to himself, thinking about how best to defeat her if she is armed. He had to get the high ground.

He reached the end of the road where it appeared washed out, perhaps from an earlier summer storm. The edge was littered with the remains of a broken barrier, only recently broken. It looked perhaps as though some vehicle that driven through it. Andrew cautiously walked up to it, rifle at the ready, checking his perimeter every few moments with a subtle style and an eerie sort of coolness. He looked as if he was born to battle. He approached the edge and peered over. There he saw shattered and upside down the pickup Caroline had procured. He started scanning around for any sight of Caroline to ensure she was dead and not hiding as was his hidden hope, wanting so badly to put a 30-06 through her skull. Crackle, he heard a noise from the left, a faint crackle in the brush and instinctively dropped himself to the ground and rolled over with weapon in hand to face the brush from whence came the noise. He heard a draw and pump click from a shot gun but no gun fired and he caught a quick glimpse of Caroline from whence he fired a shot, a loud deep "boom" whose round just barely hit the edge of tree next her. The miss was intentional. She jumped back and tripped on the dead brush and fell over. He could hear her continue to struggle with the weapon when he made the decision to bolt and run into the brush in the opposite direction, up the hill. He threw himself full force into the brush and clawed his way up the hill rapidly with his weapon slung securely over his shoulder. Finally, he heard a shot, like a loud firecracker go off and almost instantaneous heard the brush breaking before him. Another shot was fired and again he heard ahead of him the crackling of brush as the shot cut its way through the woods. He struggled some more and finally ran into a gully that provided him good track to run on. He cut into it and continued his uphill climb when he started to hear Caroline swearing at him, "I will kill you, you motherfucker. I am going to kill you! I did not give you permission to live, you celibate bitch!"

Andrew looked over for a moment and taunted her back saying, "Run girl, run. See if you beat me up the hill."

Andrew lunged himself into a clearing, cutting to the right into a group of trees. He hid behind one is ready to rifle and turned to look down the hill. Caroline was struggling up and slipping in the snow and icy limbs. He bared down the rifle and drew a bead on Caroline's head and taunted her some more, saying, "So, is this how you plan to conquer me. Is this how you plan to take possession of me. Do you think you own me you stupid fucking bitch!"

Caroline cried out like a demon, "I own you! I fucking own you bitch! I will kill you!"

Quickly Andrew moved his sight to another branch next to her. Pulling the trigger a loud crack shot through the forest and exploded the limb next Caroline. She fell back and out of sight with the sound of breaking branches in her wake. Again, Andrew bolted further up the hill. Quickly it got so steep that he had to pull himself up limb by limb. He started to tire and his body was in pain but this was the price to pay for life, this was what he had to endure to exist. He screamed at himself to go on, "Move you fool, move it if you want to live. The hell with pain! I will live, I will live!" So he carried himself further and further up the hill. Suddenly he heard another crack and, in the distance ahead of him, more breaking branches as a slug shattered some distant wood.

Then, the steep hill begun to crest and the path was more manageable, the brush had begun to thin out. Andrew found yet another gully; ran into it to get a better footing and run faster to the top. Suddenly, he slipped a patch of ice and fell hard against the ground, flat on his chest, having the wind knocked out of his chest. There he lay flat on the ground, writhing in suffocating pain. He willed himself to turn over and prepare for battle as he struggled to get some air into his empty lungs. Finally, with his senses returning he righted himself up. He pointed his rifle down the hill at the horizon, expecting Caroline to jump from brush in a cinematic scramble to destroy him, ready to pounce on him like a tiger, but he saw nothing. There was no sign of her, just the wilderness. He was tired and collapsed again on the ground, falling down and landing on his butt. Survival is not so easy, and danger is a most persistent enemy. It seems like every instinct told him to lay low and wait, to rest and relax to take it easy for once but something inside him knew better. After a few seconds of collecting his thoughts he stood up

slowly and his legs began to move, first backwards, then turning
around and continuing to the top of the hill. The stroll turned into a
walk, and his walk rapidly into a jog, his jog into a run towards the
top. He did not know why he had to get to the top of the hill, he did
not know why he had to summit but something inside reminded him
what he said to himself before, "get to the high ground!"
Something, his choice, his choice to live and grow; his choice to go
on drove him higher and higher up the hill. He forgot about his
fatigue, but he remembered life. "I will not let you down, I will
survive," he declared to himself, rallying every last bit of strength
that was in him.

It was getting late now, and the clearing afternoon skies had
begun to turn towards sunset. The eastern hills began fade into the
sky as another shade of gray and they darken. Andrew turned again
to check his six and see if Caroline was rearing her ugly head over
the horizon. A little cracking of the leaves and the swearing of her
filthy mouth, she had made her appearance finally. He aimed and
fired just ahead of her, forcing her to again fall back. She was a
pathetic creature now, struggling to get to him in her ragged,
bloodied clothes. Again, Andrew taunted her, "Come on, you lazy
bitch. Hurry the fuck up if you want to catch up to me!"

Andrew again bolted further up the hill, his superior
athleticism aiding him. He heard another shot and again it missed
badly, and lastly another shot that almost made its mark, shattering a
little sapling next to him as he made his climb. He could feel his
lungs burning, his soul wrenching and he continued up the hill.
Finally he reached the top of the hill and a clearing. He ran at full
speed to the clearing ahead, fully expecting another slope down
when suddenly he stopped!

Behold a cliff and a solid hundred-foot drop to the rocks
below. He tottered for a moment, sawing back and forth in terror
and yelled, "I will live!" And with a mighty thrust from his legs he
managed to balance himself and he fell back to the ground on his
ass. He looked ahead and saw the sun, illuminating the west. In
awe he said, "Oh my God." A blast and sudden plume of dirt kicked

up next to him and he realized it was Caroline firing at him, and this time she only just missed by inches with a deer slug. He rolled over and in one motion grabbed the Garand with his left hand and drew a bead. She was running towards him with shotgun in hand, no more than a hundred fifty feet away. Andrew's eyes followed the trigger and, in a second's time, aimed and shot the weapon right off her hands. She grabbed her right hand in agony, letting out a howl and fell over on the ground.

Andrew got up immediately and ran over to her, just twenty yards ahead. As he reached her, she got up suddenly with the already bloody knife she had holstered and tried to slice upwards at him, but he dodged and hit her hard in the face with the butt stock of the rifle. She fell over again and kicked him on his shin in return, causing him to fall over and lose the rifle, pushing the safety forward in the process. Caroline quickly picked herself up, her face bloodied and seething in hatred, pain and anger. She showed her teeth in anger and panted like a wild beast. She pounced on the rifle and rolled over to face Andrew and pulled the trigger, but the gun would not fire. She pulled the trigger again but it only half clicked. She was frustrated as Andrew stopped being motionless and lunged at her for the weapon. He grabbed both ends of the rifle and shoved it in her face causing her to fall over, but she did not let go of the weapon. Andrew fell over with her and continued to struggle for the weapon. She kicked him in the crotch with her knee as they were down still rolling around in the ground; Andrew let go in agony as she quickly picked herself up and ran out towards the clearing to get a better shot of Andrew. Andrew slowly picked himself up in pain, the knee to the crotch knocked the wind out of him almost and left a bad taste in his mouth. Caroline stood just a few feet away from the ledge and struggled to get the rifle to fire, she had no clue how to remove the safety. Andrew in pain got up and ran out towards Caroline and tackled her hard to ground as she struggled with that weapon, reaching low and grabbing her by the knees and picking her up like a wrestler before dropping her hard on the frozen ground.

She lost the weapon at that moment which Andrew was quick to grab and staggered back away from her and the ledge. She looked over momentarily and realized where she was, on the edge of the cliff. She looked away, not daring to see the light of the setting sun. As sun got lower in the sky now, the distant mountains of the Catskills drew a long dark shadow over the valley below. Her once luscious body was broken, covered in her own blood. Her nose and mouth bleeding profusely. Andrew himself was covered in it too, but not as extensively. In pain, but willing, Andrew aimed for her head as the rays of the setting sun pierced the last of the parting clouds and shown their glory. Caroline was but a shadow of darkness, an eclipse to it. Behind, the valley below was darkening and looking more like an abyss.

Andrew flipped off the safety and drew a bead on her. He remarked to her coldly and determined, "Thank God, I know how to use a gun and you don't. This weapon shall never shed innocent blood."

Bloody and in pain, her face disfigured with blood and dirt, Caroline staggered back another step slowly and looked at Andrew with her bloodied evil eyes. She now stood against the cliff.

Andrew took a step closer and continued more forcefully, "It's over Bitch! It's over. What are you going to do now? I am going to take you down and they are going to put you in jail. You won't be able to do as you want, you won't be able to fuck around with people as you please."

With a muffled scream from injury she shrieked at him, "Fuck you, you won't even fuck me, fag."

Holding the rifle more tightly and squeezing down on the trigger, Andrew retorted, "Bitch, I wouldn't fuck you if my life depended on it, you sick, psychotic bitch. God you're disgusting."

"God, God, what fucking God, you dumbshit. There is no God, there is no nothing! There is only me, I AM GOD, YOU SON OF A BITCH!"

"In your dreams, bitch," Andrew protested as loudly as he could without losing authority in his voice.

Caroline began laughing, an unnatural laugh as she moved back a little more. Her laughter soon turned to sorrow as she looked down at her bloody hands and brought them up to her face and in a muffled cry yelled, "I'm not beautiful any more, I'm not anything anymore, I can't do what I want anymore." She cried, "This can't be. I can't go to jail. I can't be stopped!" Not daring to turn around and face the light of the setting sun she bore down her eyes on Andrew and with the fury of a hell spawn demon, opened up with a vicious smile, a satanic grin with her remaining teeth in the most unnatural manner, "I will die!" And, so, she took one last step back and fell into the abyss.

With his weapons still ready he heard the distant breaking of branches and bone. He lowered his weapon and walked closer to the edge and stood straight up to bear witness to the light of the setting sun. He stood there silent and motionless as a breeze came over and rattled his coat against his sentinel body as the final rays of sun warmed him. There he beheld creation, and stood up above the darkness. He has chosen to live and the light illuminates him.

JOHN FRANCIS

The author, John Francis, hails from the Sound shore of
Westchester from his early life, with forays overseas in his
youth. Following a mostly Catholic education in
Westchester, notably in White Plains, he furthered his
education in technical and mathematical studies in college.
His life has taken him on an unexpected twenty-year
detour in Central New York where he has had multiple
careers. Along with his continued self-education in
philosophy, theology and a life-long passion for history,
he has informed his Catholic worldview. He currently still
resides in Central New York.

All authors are beholden to their readers for the books bought, appreciated and shared. Please spread the word by putting a review on the Amazon book page for this and all books that you enjoy. The authors will be grateful.